KU-995-714

This
If it is
by p
due f

The Man Who Was Not
Himself

By the same author

THREE FOR ADVENTURE
FOUR FIND DANGER
TWO MEET TROUBLE
HEIR TO MURDER
MURDER COMES HOME
WHO SAW HIM DIE?
MURDER BY THE WAY
FOUL PLAY SUSPECTED
WHO DIED AT THE
    GRANGE?
FIVE TO KILL
MURDER AT KING'S
    KITCHEN
WHO SAID MURDER?
CRIME WITH MANY
    VOICES
NO CRIME MORE CRUEL
MURDER MAKES MURDER
MYSTERY MOTIVE
FIRST A MURDER
LEND A HAND TO
    MURDER
OUT OF THE SHADOWS
DEATH OUT OF DARKNESS
CAT AND MOUSE
MURDER AT END HOUSE
RUNAWAY
DEATH OF A STRANGER
MURDER ASSURED
MISSING FROM HOME

THICKER THAN WATER
HOW MANY TO KILL?
GO AHEAD WITH MURDER
THE MAN I KILLED
THE EDGE OF TERROR
HATE TO KILL
THE QUIET FEAR
GUILT OF INNOCENCE

The Fane Brothers books

TAKE A BODY
LAME DOG MURDER
MURDER IN THE STARS
MAN ON THE RUN

The Dr. Cellini books

CUNNING AS A FOX
WICKED AS THE DEVIL
SLY AS A SERPENT
CRUEL AS A CAT
TOO GOOD TO BE TRUE
A PERIOD OF EVIL
AS LONELY AS THE
    DAMNED
AS EMPTY AS HATE
AS MERRY AS HELL
THIS MAN DID I KILL?

The Man Who Was Not Himself

The 11th story of Dr. Emmanuel Cellini

by

John Creasey

as Michael Halliday

HODDER AND STOUGHTON
LONDON SYDNEY AUCKLAND TORONTO

390112 C

Class

Copyright © 1976 by the estate of John Creasey. First printed 1976.
ISBN 0 340 20960 7. All rights reserved. No part of this publication
may be reproduced or transmitted in any form or by any means,
electronic or mechanical, including photocopy, recording, or any
information storage and retrieval system, without permission in
writing from the publisher. Printed in Great Britain for Hodder and
Stoughton Limited, London by The Garden City Press Limited,
Letchworth, Hertfordshire SG6 1JS.

Contents

CITY OF LONDON
LIBRARIES

1

The Waking

HE WOKE TO strange noises.

They were strange only in the sense that they were unfamiliar; a woman, somewhere nearby, was singing; a man, farther away, was saying 'Good morning'. There were other trifles of noise, too, which he did not recognise; a squeak, the bark of a small dog, the noise of a car engine.

He heard these sounds while his eyes were still closed.

And he heard the splashing of water, as of a shower.

He was — he must be dreaming.

Slowly, he opened his eyes, to a room he had never seen before.

It was a pleasant room, with large birds on the wallpaper and pastel blue paint on the half-closed door, through which the sound of splashing water was coming. The furniture was of light-coloured oak or birch, nice enough, but — he had never seen it before.

He was on a huge bed.

It was one of the largest beds he had ever seen — seeming to stretch far beyond him in all directions. On one side, above unfamiliar yellow sheets and an unfamiliar cellular blanket, was a pillow with a dent, the kind of dent likely to be made by a head.

A *woman*?

If he had any doubts, they were dispelled at once, for

a quick look round showed him a host of feminine things; toiletries, brushes, and a filmy dressing jacket. He stared at them, so mesmerised that he was oblivious of different sounds; the water still splashing, brisk sounds of rubbing, followed by footsteps. Next moment, a woman stepped into the room.

True, she wore a gaily-patterned towelling dressing-gown or robe; but it flew open with what he thought of as a lamentable casualness, leaving nothing at all to the imagination. It was a long time before he really studied her face. It seemed to him that she was quite oblivious of the fact that she was being watched. Not glancing towards him, or acknowledging his existence by a flicker of an eyelash, she began to take things out of the drawer of a chest; stockings, a brassiere, a slip, tossing them over the back of a nearby chair.

Then, at last, she did look at him; and momentarily, she was startled.

"My! I *am* having an effect on Tizzy this morning!"

Tizzy! Was she calling him Tizzy?

She slid the robe off her shoulders and let it slide; such a tiny waist; such —

As she turned more fully towards him he noticed that the deep valley between her breasts was golden-tanned — and that, for the first time, she frowned, as if there were something she didn't understand. At last, at *last*, she must have realised that the man in her bed was a stranger.

But perhaps she had known it all along.

Then who was she?

A prostitute?

She drew closer and said: "Neil, are you all right?"

His name wasn't Neil, it was Hugh.

She leaned over him.

Any second now she was going to realise what a mistake she had made.

"Neil," she said, "you're only half-awake. Did you have a bad dream?"

Dream? This was all a dream — all, that is, but the feeling that was beginning to stir in him.

"I'll soon drive it away," she said.

Without a hint of warning, with a speed which surely told of having done just this before, she drew her arms round him.

He lost his head, accepting the strength and knowledge and passion in her; in them both.

She was not beautiful. But she had a lovely skin and fine, honey-brown eyes with long lashes. Her hair was rather charmingly untidy, and the same colour as her eyes.

"Darling," she said.

"Yes?" His voice. Whatever else failed surely his voice must give him away.

"You'll be late."

"Sure about that?"

"You've missed the eight fifty already."

He glanced at a bedside clock, a pretty thing of porcelain with birds all about it; the time was half past eight.

"I suppose I have," he admitted.

His voice. Why didn't she realise that there was something different about his voice?

"You look so smug — let me guess. Percy is going to give you a lift this morning."

"I made no plans," he answered.

"Then the boss has given you a morning off."

So he had a 'boss'.

"Have you ever known him do such a thing?"

"He has not changed."

"Then darling, it's very clear that you must get up."

"Ah," he said. "It couldn't be Saturday or Sunday, could it?"

"If it were, you'd know," she said. "The children wouldn't have let you slug-a-bed."

My God: *children.*

His feeling of astonishment and unbelief were so great that surely she could not fail to see it; but that was the moment when the telephone bell rang. It was close to his ear, behind him, and she, still lying by his side, plucked up the telephone, saying:

"This is Grace Powell."

His name was Buckingham; Hugh Buckingham.

She laughed, and he could feel her body quivering.

"*Really*, darling." There were a few moments of silence before she went on: "Yes, I'd love to come and have coffee and you can tell me all the details, but I'm in a hurry now — Neil's late and I've got to shoot him off. 'Bye, then. What time? Eleven o'clock? Lovely!" She rang off, and then kissed the tip of his nose. "You'll be late," she declared.

"Could I take the day off?"

"No, you could not — it's risky enough getting in late."

"Yes," he admitted. "Pity."

He kissed her right eyebrow.

"But I wish you could," she said. "It would be — "

"Remember eleven," he interrupted.

"Eleven? Oh, Roberta! I could easily ring her up and put her off."

"Such a sacrifice, for me?"

She said mischievously: "If we had time, and we haven't, *could* you command a repeat performance?"

At first, he didn't understand; and it was only when he saw her flush a little that he realised what she meant. And on the instant he was in the grip of temptation. His hands actually gripped her arms and his body tensed. What stopped him, he did not really know. A sense of decency; a sense that he should not take advantage of this anomalous — what a word but what other was there? — situation again. A sense that afterwards, when she came to know the truth it would be bad for her to accept: a 'repeat performance' would be unbearable.

"Grace," he said. "I hate to say it, but I *must* catch that next train."

She sprang up.

"I'll get your breakfast before I dress. You've fifteen minutes to shower and shave."

She blew him a kiss as she danced away, and now he began to act quickly.

Everything was easy for him.

What a lucky man this Neil Powell was!

Towel by the bath, soap in the dishes, socks and underwear in a dressing-room outside the bathroom, suit, tie, accessories, shoes, on or near a chair all ready; anyone could have finished in time. He glanced at himself in the mirror of the bedroom dressing-table: yes, he was exactly the same, he remembered himself quite well.

Grace called: "Breakfast on the table!"

"Coming!" he answered.

She had cooked bacon and eggs. There was a toaster on a small table by his side, which told him that Neil liked his toast hot. A green porcelain coffee pot was percolating away, *bubble-bubble, toil and trouble*. Grace sat down and poured out two cups.

"Or would my lord and master like to eat alone?" she asked gaily.

He said soberly: "Sweetheart, you look very good this morning."

To his surprise — for she had accepted so much without question — this seemed to puzzle her. She said quietly:

"Do you know you haven't called me that in years."

This was the moment, of course, when he should have told her everything. That he had never seen her before, that he was what his father would have called a 'cad', that he was completely baffled, and could explain nothing — including the fact that he did not know who he was supposed to be, where the train he was to catch was going, where he worked, what he did.

Perhaps, he told himself not only then but later, that might have been the wisest and kindest course to take. Only one thing stopped him: the expression in her eyes as he had called her sweetheart. Only one thing? Well, there was another; he wanted to find out how this strange thing had happened.

And another still: he did not expect ever to see her again, and deep within him was a strange reluctance to bring this about.

The real Neil would return and might be, could only be, baffled by some of her questions, but she would probably put it down to a change of mind. It was the coward's way out yet he persuaded himself that it was the kind, the gallant way. And so he simply pressed her hand, and ate, and drank, until suddenly she cried:

"You *must* go, Neil."

So he sprang up; and he put his arms round her and kissed her.

He sensed that this was one of the happiest mornings of her life, and he was both touched and glad.

Once outside, walking in the same direction as several men dressed for city offices, he made another, shattering discovery.

It had been one of the happiest mornings of his life, too.

2

The Office

"WHAT I FIRST need to do," Hugh Buckingham told himself, "is think."

He was walking along an unfamiliar main road, apparently in a suburb of London, for there were the big red London Transport buses and, far off, a tube station. Men from other streets, obviously white-collar workers of a superior position or they would not be going to work so late, appeared to be heading for the tube station, and doubtless he would be expected to catch the next business train from there.

But to where?

It did not really matter whether he got to this office, of which he knew nothing, on time. Indeed, it did not greatly matter if he got there at all, except —

The first dangerous — or acknowledged-to-be-dangerous — thought, entered his head. Unless he did go to the office what was the chance of seeing Grace again? For unless he went to the office, how could he expect to find out more about himself? Quite suddenly he gave a snort of laughter which made a young woman pushing a pram look at him in surprise.

He could go back to her house, of course: but if he went back — supposing Neil opened the door?

He rocked with laughter.

"Mr. Neil Powell, I presume."

"No, sir, you are mistaken. *You* are Mr. Neil Powell."

Stop this nonsense and get on with the thinking, he adjured himself, and yet at the same time he was pleased — delighted — that despite the shock of finding himself in this extraordinary predicament, he could see the funny side of it. But he must think. And only an addlepated idiot, having started to think about the situation, would go on from here — office, the real Neil, even Grace, sweet Grace, passionate Grace, must be put out of his mind. This was the common-sense result of thinking; but he scowled.

He was not far from the tube station.

Where should he —

Great Scott. *Think*! He took out a wallet which he had known to be in the inside jacket pocket but which he hadn't looked at. As he took the wallet out another thought struck him with a kind of nauseating body blow: a fact. *The clothes he wore were his own.* The wallet was completely unfamiliar.

He opened the wallet, and found a season ticket from Gretel Wood, S.W. to Charing Cross. Gretel Wood he had never heard of, but Charing Cross he knew as well as the back of his hand. He checked: this was a twelve-month ticket and the month was June, so he knew where to get on and where to get off.

A small crowd was now converging on Gretel Wood, as if in a form of invasion. The guard at the top of the steps was clipping some and examining other tickets. An illuminated sign said:

Next train: Aldgate East. 9.27

Immediately beneath this was a dial with a square white face and stark black numerals, reading: *9.24*.

Charing Cross, but where in Charing —

"Hallo, Neil. You're for the high jump too, are you?"

A man of about his own age, ginger-haired, bowler-hatted, carrying a furled umbrella, slapped him on the shoulder. He spun round.

"Er — yes, I suppose so."

"You *suppose* so," boomed the other. "Up to his eyes in work, and two of his bright boys late! Old Pebble will have a fit. Got a good excuse?"

Before he could think what to answer a roar of sound drowned most of the other noises on the platform: the oncoming train. "Should be about right here," said the other man, and gripped his arm. The train glided in, and stopped with automatic doors sliding apart immediately in front of them. "Plenty of room. There's always plenty of room on *this* train — not that I make a habit of catching it! Ha! Ha!" He led the way towards the seats and they sat down.

"Well?" asked Ginger. "Have you?"

Curse the man's persistence!

"Have I what?"

"Say, you're a bit dim this morning! You feeling all right? Haven't got one of your old headaches coming on, have you?"

Think.

He needed an excuse for being late. He, Hugh Buck — no! He, Neil Powell, was in so humble a position that he needed to placate his boss if he were an hour late. What, and where, was it? Why didn't he do the obvious and sensible thing, say his headache was so bad that he ought to get off at the next station and vanish? Never to be seen by Ginger — or Grace — again.

Think.

"I have a hell of a headache," he declared, but his head had never felt clearer, no matter how confused his mind might be.

"I hope they're not coming back," said Ginger, as if genuinely concerned. "I'll tell you what, Neil. If you show up looking absolutely groggy Old Pebby will give you full marks for trying. He's bound to send you home.

And I — ah — I could say I felt I ought not to leave you unaccompanied. Get me off the hook, too." After a long pause during which Ginger looked hopefully at Hugh Buckingham and Hugh half-closed his eyes and looked nowhere in particular, Ginger went on: "You don't mind my asking, do you?"

"Of course not," Hugh said. "Good of you."

"Good of *you*. I say — would you care to sit back and not talk, while I skim through the old Tel? Talk if you'd rather."

"No, you read," Hugh insisted, and sat back closing his eyes, devoutly thankful for this small respite. *Think*, he adjured himself. It was a damned peculiar situation in every way, and he simply could not go on with it. On the other hand —

What a soft and yielding bosom she had.

Grace.

And apart from that, there was the adventurous side that appealed to him. How long could he keep the deception up? Deception? Of course it was a deception, what else could one possibly call it? If he could pass muster with other men with whom Neil Powell worked day in and day out, then it would amount to a miracle. But the ginger-haired man did not suspect for a moment; he, too, had accepted not only his face but his voice! That was surely the most utterly astonishing fact. A double one could, by stretching one's imagination to the limit, imagine getting away with; but a double with an identical voice, one which two people who 'knew' him accepted without question, was beyond imagination.

What harm could come through going on with the next stage? And learning yet more about 'himself'—who he was, what he did? And it was almost as if luck was going his way; the fortuitous meeting with Ginger for instance, who could lead him to his very office, knew the names of his associates. He smothered another chuckle: someone there was bound to find out.

"I say, old boy." Ginger lowered his *Daily Telegraph.* "Are you all right? Not going to be sick or anything, are you?"

"Just — er — ah — hiccoughed," explained Hugh.

"Oh. Good. You don't look too bobbish, you know. A bit pale. *Sure* you feel all right?"

"Shouldn't we let Old Pebble decide?" suggested Hugh.

"Eh? Let old — damned good idea," agreed Ginger, with a half-snort of laughter. He went back to his newspaper without further comment until, without once having glanced away, he folded it neatly and placed it inside his briefcase. "Well, here we are, old boy. Better be at the gates, get ahead of the rush. Eh?"

Inside the lid of the briefcase in gilt lettering was the name: *Arthur Cecil Thwaites.*

The train stopped, the doors opened, and: "Here we go!" cried Arthur Cecil Thwaites, and he sprang out and raced towards an exit and what proved to be an escalator; they were so far ahead of the crowd that they had it almost to themselves. Soon they were out of Charing Cross Station, Villiers Street ahead of them, Temple Gardens bright with tulips inviting them to their right, the old and mammoth buildings of Whitehall Place to their left, and more embankment gardens as well as the so far invisible Thames. It was hard to realise that so many places of such beauty, so much historic architecture, so many flowers tended by the hand of man, could be approached by this little backyard of a street with a dark and menacing bridge overhead.

Which way would they go?

Hugh Buckingham, who had never gone in for practised deceit and would have called himself a law-abiding citizen, staggered as if losing his balance. Thwaites grabbed him. Ginger-haired, freckled, Arthur Cecil Thwaites had long fingers with the clutch of steel.

"I say, old man, are you — "

"I'm sorry, I stumbled."

"The sooner you're on your way home the better it'll be," declared Thwaites, and still holding him firmly led him towards the right, and what was presently shown to be a modern monstrosity of glass and reinforced concrete.

Did they work here?

On the wall as they entered, passing eight narrow steps, was a peculiarly inept example of the stone-mason's craft: *Department of Overseas Trade — Special Services.* The stonemason had fashioned the words with an over-ornate lettering that took time to read. By now impatient, Thwaites said:

"Come *on*, old boy."

'Come on' led to a bleak foyer, supervised by half a dozen attendants. The foyer echoed to the solemnity of a dozen 'Good mornings' as the lift took the two men with surprising speed to the fourteenth floor.

"I hope to heaven," whispered Thwaites, "that he's in a good mood."

Who was this Pebble; this tyrant; this man who seemed to have the power of a king maker? The first door to their right was opening slowly. On it was a brass plate bearing the name: *Nathaniel D. Pebblewhite.* Beyond were a number of smaller offices and beyond these a huge glass-walled main office where could be seen at least a hundred desks and as many typewriters and perhaps twice as many telephones. Yet if noise came from them it seemed to stop suddenly at Nathaniel D. Pebblewhite's opening door.

He stood there, strangely isolated.

Greying hair, sideburns, a thin, almost fleshless nose, he could not, by any standard, have been considered a goodlooking man.

"Good morning," he said, and his voice held the false

gentleness of sarcasm. "We have been hoping you would come."

"Mr. Pebblewhite," Thwaites said very quickly, "I'm not sure Mr. Powell *should* have come. I met him soon after we started out and he's not well — palpably not well," added Thwaites, as if 'palpably' would clinch the matter then and there.

Pebblewhite stared at Hugh Buckingham through a pair of meanly-cut *pince-nez*.

While Pebblewhite scrutinised, Thwaites fidgeted, and some hundred men and women looked on with interest. Something was stirring inside Buckingham, revolt against such obviously tyrannical control as this man exerted; one had only to imagine him turning to the spectators and in a sharp, incisive voice say: "Get to work," to see their eyes instantly lowered to their desks.

But thought of revolt was absurd.

Pebblewhite was examining him so closely that Hugh felt his deception must instantly be laid bare.

Instead, a frosty voice declaimed: "If you are not well, Powell, it was most praiseworthy of you to come in. I suggest you stay for an hour, or possibly two, and if you are then incapable of concentrated thought, you may go home. There will be no need to consult me further."

He turned back into his richly carpeted office, and the door closed behind him. For a few seconds there was silence; no one but he and Thwaites moved and no one spoke. But at the closing of Pebblewhite's door, there was a surge forward, and suddenly he was surrounded by girls, young women, older women.

"You shouldn't have come, Neil ... You *do* look ill, Neil ... You should have made him go back, Arthur ... Is it one of your old headaches, Neil? ... Would you like some tea ... Coffee? ... A whisky ... Milk ... Oh, poor Neil."

He was led by a small entourage to one of the bigger

desks near a window, and a chair was pulled back for him. It was a moment of guilt in a period of subdued Bedlam; because he wasn't Neil Powell.

What would they do, what would they say, if he jumped up and cried:

"My name is Hugh Buckingham. I have never heard of Neil Powell."

Suddenly, a thought as to what they would do came to his mind, and he could both have laughed and cried.

It would clinch his assertion that he was ill. More, they would probably decide that he had gone queer in the head.

3

'Work'

HE SAT AT the desk, and a long-haired blonde hovered, placing writing pads, pens and a variety of oddments about the desk. From time to time she touched him or brushed against him, and while he felt sure much of this was deliberate, it was not seductive; but there wasn't much doubt she was fond of him.

He nearly jumped out of his seat at the implication! *Fond* of him? Fond of Neil Powell — that someone as close, and in daily contact, was fooled so easily shocked him.

"And you won't stay if you don't feel like it, will you?" she asked.

"No," promised Hugh, faintly. "You have my word for that."

At last she left him, for a desk along an aisle where she could see him but he could not see her without turning round. On his right, at a similar desk and with similar card indexes and loose leaf ledgers, was a man with a slightly humped back; he was very intent on his work; for that matter everybody was; Pebblewhite certainly had this department under tight control. On the pretext of opening ledgers and checking files, Hugh watched what the other was doing; and very soon he realised what the job was. On the card indexes were

sets of figures, giving details of goods. The headings
ran:

Date Article Quantity Order Order Ack'd Entered in
Rec'd Filled   Ledger

and at the bottom was the name and address of the firm
concerned and a similar lot of headings:

Firm   Category   Address Personnel County
Ordering   if known

His job, then, was to enter the items from these cards
to the loose leaf ledgers: and then he saw that the
right-hand side of the ledger had to do with payment,
credit arrangements, banks — everything else to do with
a single transaction. Here, the names of the firms were
at the top and some firms had several filled sheets:
hence the use of the loose-leaf system.

All the loose-leaf entries were made in ink.

He picked up one of the pens. He assured himself
that he knew what to do — and then he had another
shock. All the handwriting on the sheets he had so far
seen was the same. He checked a dozen more and found
this to be true: the rule must be one ledger one man.
But the handwriting was not his.

He sat, pen in hand, staring. Here was the end, then;
he simply could not keep on with the pretence. He had
only to make one entry to reveal the impersonation.
Ah! That was a word which hadn't occurred to him
before but which was unquestionably the right one. He
was impersonating Neil Powell; and he must stop
at once. He had actually pushed his chair back, when
his telephone bell rang. It was so subdued that at first
he didn't realise that it was his, but an impatient glance
from the man across the aisle left him in no doubt. He
lifted the receiver, and announced:

"Neil Powell speaking."

"Oh, Neil," a woman said. "I was so worried when I

heard you weren't in this morning, I felt that I just had
to ring again. How are you? You *did* just miss the
train, didn't you? I mean, you are all right?"

"Oh, I'm fine," Hugh said.

"Oh, thank goodness! Then we can still have lunch?"

Lunch? With a strange woman who had a somewhat
languorous and at the same time not unattractive voice.
He had no idea what she looked like or where he was
to meet her. The very thought of lunching with her was
impossible.

But —

This sounded like an *affaire,* and if anyone could see
through the impersonation then a mistress could. Oh, be
honest! If he could contrive to meet her he might find
out more about Grace Powell.

Face it, he urged himself: admit it. *I want to know
more about Grace.*

"Darling," the woman said, "are you there?"

"Yes," said Hugh hastily. "Someone was passing —
I've done the most ridiculous thing, I've lost my notes
about when and where. I mean — "

"You *are* woolgathering this morning," the woman
said, and there was an edge to the laughter in her voice.
"The usual time, darling —" She paused, and he held
his breath for that told him nothing at all. "One fifteen
at Simpsons. You *can* come, can't you?" she added
eagerly or anxiously. "You aren't — "

Someone cut them off.

He had no idea whether it was the switchboard
operator here or the automatic control by some faceless
computer; he only knew that the line went dead, and
he stared at the mouthpiece stupidly before putting it
down. One fifteen at Simpsons — what did that tell him?
He was too bemused to think clearly, and all he felt
like doing was getting up and walking out. He dared

not make an entry in the ledger, he dared not keep a luncheon appointment with a woman he didn't know — damn it, whose *name* he didn't know. The whole situation was utterly impossible and the quicker he became Hugh Buckingham, bachelor — well, long-time widower — and returned to his pleasant apartment in Chelsea and forgot this strange trip into fantasy —

He drew in a hissing breath.

Could that be the explanation? More fantasy?

Nonsense. Neil Powell *alias* — no! Hugh Buckingham and Neil Powell both existed. There was ample proof of it.

Wasn't there?

A shadow appeared, and the blonde looked at him anxiously. She touched his shoulder, and was about to speak when a man pushed past, saying: "What ho, Sylvia, you might try looking at *me* like that sometime."

Sylvia!

She ignored the remark, keeping her fingers on his shoulder while looking into his face with great intensity. He thought what a pretty thing she was, with her lovely eyes of china blue, and silky, pale-gold hair.

"Neil," she said, "I have to go to lunch early today. I'm meeting a friend. Will you give up and let me see you to the station — or better still," she added, "a taxi."

He hesitated, then pressed her hand with his.

"Why, yes. Bless you."

She coloured brightly but did not look away.

"A quarter of an hour?"

"I must say," said the hunch-backed man across the aisle, "you look remarkably fit for a sick man. I suppose you know that *I* shall have to stay late for at least three nights to make up for the work you will have failed to do. You may fool Pebblewhite but you don't fool *me* with your philandering."

He had turned his head, revealing a thin, over-lined face and the most amazingly big, hooded brown eyes.

His mouth had a bitter twist as he indicated the ledgers stacked on his desk.

If only I knew his name, thought Hugh.

The man was actually quivering with repressed rage.

Hugh said, awkwardly: "I do know how you feel and I know it's damned unfair. But I really am in an extremely difficult spot today. I'm not simply sneaking out for a pleasant lunch or even for— " He broke off, as two people passed, and then continued: "I'm sorry. I'll try to make it up to you."

The hunchback had turned his swivel chair round to look at him squarely. Something in what Hugh had said obviously surprised and, what was more, touched him. His quivering stopped and his manner and voice softened.

"Oh, I see. I didn't realise there was — there was anything serious. Don't take any notice of me, Neil. It's old Pebblewhite, really. He doesn't seem to think anyone else in the office is capable of working overtime. He always seems to think a man like me is lucky to — oh, never mind, never mind. I'm sorry."

He swung his chair back almost savagely to his desk and began to work furiously.

Hugh stood up, frowning; he did not understand this place and there was really no reason why he ever should, but he felt an overwhelming sense of injustice and of anger against Pebblewhite. He stared at the page he had not even touched, and then suddenly a thought entered his head and he leaned forward and peered along the aisle, behind him. Four, or was it five, desks back was Thwaites, talking to a tall, dark girl. Hugh got up and went towards him. The girl moved away, while Thwaites said with quick and superficial concern:

"I say, old chap, are you sure you ought still to be here?"

"No," answered Hugh. "I'm going almost at once,

Sylvia's seeing me to the station. But I'm in rather a spot, old boy. I wondered if you could help me out."

"Glad to," promised Thwaites, warmly. "Just name it."

"Well, the trouble is" — he nodded towards the hunch-backed man — "he's had three extra ledgers thrown at him for tonight, and now it looks as if he'll get mine. I wondered if you could spare an evening or two — just a couple of hours, to — "

Thwaites could cry off, very quickly; he could be very apologetic but have an inescapable engagement; he could even give a grudging consent, feeling that he had been trapped into saying yes. He did none of these things, but gripped Hugh's arm with those surprisingly strong fingers, beamed broadly, and said as if with heartfelt thanks:

"Help out old Torino? Delighted, old boy. Absolutely delighted. Just do one thing for me in return, will you?" He winked a broad, slow, conspiratorial wink, and squeezed tightly enough to hurt. "Telephone Maggie for me this afternoon, will you? Say *you* asked me to work late to help you out. You know Maggie! She considers me the oracle of all liars and you a little George Washington. Thanks, old chap!"

Hugh went back to his desk, left everything tidy, saw Sylvia coming along the aisle and glanced at Torino's bowed head. Did one 'Mister' Torino? Better not risk it. He said: "I hope you won't think I'm interfering, but I've asked Arthur Thwaites if he could sit in for me for a couple of nights, and he's going to."

Torino turned slowly, pen poised in hand, looked up, moistened his lips, and then said in a cracked voice:

"You are very kind. Thank you."

To Hugh it looked almost as if the little man was about to cry. It was a strange moment as Torino turned away. Then Sylvia drew up, carrying a shoulder-strap bag, and they went out of the big office, past the private ones, and eventually to the lifts. Several people were waiting. Neither spoke until they were out of the foyer walking down those narrow steps.

Then, Sylvia asked: "Is Doreen getting difficult, Neil?"

Doreen.

"You know you don't have to pretend with me," Sylvia said. "Everything's going wrong, isn't it?"

"Er — in a way," Hugh muttered.

"In *every* way. Does Doreen want you to divorce your wife, now that she's free?"

"It — it wouldn't be very surprising," said Hugh evasively.

"Surprising! Neil, if you'd had just one eye half open you could have seen what was coming. Doreen — " She broke off, and then added in a quivering voice: "Neil. You *will* tell me if you think it's none of my business, won't you?"

"Yes," he promised.

"I don't know what Doreen is like as a — a lover, but she could be a harridan as a wife."

He had to say something: show some intelligent interest, so he exlaimed:

"*Doreen* could?"

"Yes. Your beautiful Doreen. And Neil — I do know her."

"I know you do."

"I wish to heaven I'd never introduced you," Sylvia said, "but I knew there was no hope for me! Sometimes I think the old, non-permissive days were best, when marriages just had to last forever." She was talking very rapidly now, as if the words hurt. "I hate to say it, but she will ruin you. For Doreen she has been quite modest up to now, the Savoy or Simpsons occasionally and some little place for an unpretentious dinner, but — she wants you, Neil. She knows it won't be too long before you come into the Powell fortune, and will she spend your money then! It sounds catty I know, but I must risk that. I care for you too much myself to stand by and watch this tragedy happen."

"Tragedy being — ?"

"Tragedy being· you having to divorce Grace, and the children having two homes which are *not* better than one, and Doreen demanding the social whirl, and Grace going out to work again because she doesn't want to be a drain on you — that's what I mean by tragedy."

By now they were walking along the embankment gardens, past massed arrays of tulips and geraniums, oblivious of the hundreds who shared the grounds with them. He could feel the intensity of this girl; the goodness which emanated from her. But never in his life had he been more anxious to meet a person than he was to meet Doreen.

"Sylvia," he said, "tell me one thing. What is it that worries you about my seeing Doreen at lunch today?"

"Oh, that's easy," she said. "I'm afraid you'll promise her you'll divorce Grace. She will pressure you, use all her feminine wiles, and does she have wiles! But don't promise her, Neil, *please.* Things may not always be perfect between you and Grace but they are heavenly compared with what they would be with Doreen."

He found himself saying almost as if he were actually Neil Powell:

"I won't make Doreen any promises, Sylvia. Don't worry at all about that."

She stared up at him, her blue eyes clouded with concern; suddenly she went up on tiptoe and kissed him on the cheek.

With a brief wave of her hand, she turned and hurried away.

4

Push?

HUGH STARED AFTER her.

She seemed now so familiar, although he had seen her only a few times and only once for more than a few moments. Of her feeling for him — for *Neil Powell* — there could be no shadow of doubt, and yet he felt that the kiss, the feeling and the fear had all been for him. She was walking quickly, and soon she was lost among the crowds of early lunch-time workers. He turned towards Savoy Hill, passing the Savoy beyond the trees on his right, seeing the narrow turning which led to the Strand not far from Simpsons.

He thought of Savoy Hill not only for the hotel but because British broadcasting had been born there; at least, the British Broadcasting Corporation had, in one of these tall, begrimed houses where the foliage of trees gave grim defiance to the despoliation of London's building. Walking, he found the incline surprisingly steep. Or was that an illusion, had he spent so much nervous energy that he was physically tired? He reached the Strand, and turned left for Simpsons.

Someone pushed him.

It wasn't a heavy push; not a shove or a heave, just a push. But he was on one foot, and in that miracle of timing the human body carried out each day — not quite on one leg, not quite off the other. So he lost his balance and swayed towards the roadway, perilously near the stream of traffic. A huge red bus passed him, touching one shoulder. He felt the jolt and the jarring through his whole body. A man's arm swung out and dragged him back to the pavement. The roar of London's traffic reached an awful crescendo, bus engines snarled, brakes screamed, his shoulder hurt like the very devil and his legs were so weak he thought they would collapse.

Voices came to him.

"Are you all right?"

"Is he hurt?"

"He looks *terrible*."

"Does he need a doctor?"

"He could have been killed."

Words burst out of him.

"Someone pushed me!"

"Don't be silly," a man said.

"He slipped."

"What about a doctor?"

A policeman's voice sounded, strong, unmistakably authoritative.

"Is someone hurt? Make way, please."

He reached Hugh.

"How do you feel, sir?"

"If I could just get to Simpsons — "

"You've an appointment there?"

"Yes, but — they've a good washroom, and — first aid. I don't think I'm hurt. I just banged into a bus."

A wag said hoarsely: "You should just see the bus!"

Someone laughed, several reproved. "This isn't funny."

"It's only a few steps along, sir," the officer said, "and if you need to go on to hospital you can do so from there."

"Thanks. I — Officer!"

They were beginning to walk, Hugh rather groggily,
as if he were using someone else's legs.

"Yes, sir?"

"Somebody pulled me back — a man. And a girl
helped."

"Slipped away in the crowd, I expect," the policeman
said. "A lot of people avoid publicity like the plague,
you know. Look around and see if you recognise them."

Hugh looked around but it was a mistake; just turning his head made him feel dizzy, and he missed a step.
The constable held the arm that had met the bus full
force, and he winced.

"Sorry, sir."

"Just bruised," said Hugh. "I really think I'll be all
right when I'm sitting down." He thought: *I was
pushed.* He wondered whether he should tell the policeman, then decided against it. It would lead to more
interrogations, more questions and the possible reason
for being pushed. He thought: *Someone tried to push
me under a bus, so someone tried to kill me.*

No. Not me.

Someone tried to kill Neil Powell, husband of Grace,
lover of Doreen.

"Here we are, sir," the constable said.

A doorman looked at him in some surprise and even
a little disdain and then said: "Mr. Powell, sir! Have
you been hurt?" Another man, smaller, dinner-jacketed,
red of face, came hurrying:

"Mr. Powell! What happened — ?"

"Is — " he began, wanting to know whether Doreen
was here yet, and then it came to him that he did not
know her surname and so could not ask for her.

"No, sir, your friend hasn't arrived," the dinner-
jacketed man declared. "She — why, here she is, sir!"

So, Doreen was coming towards him.

There was only one woman on her own, so this must

be Doreen; and he thought, through the mists of his aches and pains: she is beautiful. Not just a well-dressed, well-made-up, good-looking woman — but beautiful, in the way of Southern Europeans, with peach-coloured skin, dark, raven-black hair, brown eyes now filled with deep concern. And how she moved and what a figure she had! Men made way for her and suddenly she was in front of him with her hands stretched out in compassion. There was no hint of hardness, of rapacity, nothing which little Sylvia had led him to believe: at least, nothing visible.

"Well," she said, "what happened?"

"The gentleman had an accident," announced the policeman.

Hugh said: "It's a lot of fuss about nothing, really. I just tried to push a bus over."

"Neil, don't joke. Are you hurt? Where — "

"If I may suggest, Miss," said the man in the dinner-jacket, "we have a first-aid room with a fully qualified nurse in attendance, and if you care to go upstairs with Mr. Powell, then the nurse can advise whether a doctor is needed. Your table will be kept, of course."

An elevator was stopped, and they went upstairs. The room was pleasant and the nurse both pretty and efficient. The young policeman, who had been busy on his radio, reported with evident pleasure:

"I have authority to stay until the decision whether to summon a doctor is known."

"Good," Hugh said with forced heartiness. "But I won't need one."

"You're sure, dear?" Had Doreen's tone held a certain relief? Was it possible that she did not want a doctor?

The nurse eased first his jacket off, and then his shirt. Her examination was quick and efficient.

"So that didn't hurt?"

"Not to say hurt."

. .

"Then nothing is broken and I doubt if anything is badly sprained."

"Oh, thank goodness!" exclaimed Doreen, and this time there was no doubt whatever of her intense relief. "I'm so glad, Neil."

"You've some bad bruises," the nurse stated. "I can rub in an embrocation. It will lessen the pain, but it won't go altogether."

"What would you recommend for it?" asked Doreen.

Doreen, the flatterer; Doreen, who for some undisclosed reason did not like the nurse. There were indications that the feeling was mutual. Antipathy, Hugh thought; or could they possibly know each other?

The nurse said briskly: "I'll give you a note for the embrocation — you won't need a prescription. I'm going to put some on now and it will sting." She squeezed a pinkish-looking ointment on to the palm of her right hand and then began to rub firmly and evenly.

"Shouldn't he wear a sling?" asked Doreen.

"Nasty uncomfortable things," the nurse replied. "But you could tie a red ribbon round your arm as if you'd been vaccinated. That would make most people careful not to bump into you." She gave a quiet little smile that excluded Doreen. "Can you eat and drink with your left hand?"

"Reasonably," he answered.

"Because tomorrow and for a few days afterwards you'll probably have to."

"I suppose I'm lucky I won't have to be spoon-fed."

"*Anyone*," declared the constable, who had been so still and silent that they had forgotten he was there, "who tried to push over a London bus is lucky to be taking any nourishment at all, sir."

Everyone knew exactly what he meant: that the victim of the 'accident' was lucky to be alive.

Hugh Buckingham had no idea whether the corner

table with a sweeping view was the regular table where Powell ate with Doreen at Simpsons. If it was, then he was a big spender and probably a big tipper. He did not know whether today's service was normal, or whether a special effort was being made; but he had only to glance up for a waiter to spring forward. There were three: an Englishman, a Frenchman and an Italian.

"Coming, sir," and "at once, M'sieur", and "Si, Signor", made a refrain over and over again, through his caviare and Doreen's pâté de foie gras; through roast duckling cooked not in oranges but in grapes with a light Rhine wine, and through a lemon soufflé. They were there for two hours, and he waited with a certain trepidation for the bill. It came with the Frenchman.

"L'addition, m'sieur, à votre service."

Seventeen pounds, five shillings; with tip, twenty pounds. Not cheap but for such a superb meal, not exorbitant. He put his hand to his hip pocket for his wallet.

Supposing, just supposing, there wasn't enough in Neil Powell's wallet to meet the bill?

The Frenchman handed him a ballpoint pen which looked as if it were gold-capped.

"M'sieur, he will sign?"

Relief swept over Hugh, but the first flush had hardly come before a cold douche of dread drowned it. He could not sign Neil Powell's signature; even if the waiter were fooled, Doreen wouldn't be, and the head waiter would probably notice something different in the writing. As if he had not seen the proffered pen, he took out the wallet, and opened it, to find five — no, *six* — five pound notes.

And four would be enough.

"Darling," Doreen said, "I seem to have been talking all through the meal and you've hardly been able to get a word in edgeways, but we *will* have to think about it soon. You know what a perfectly dreadful time I had with Wilfrid, and now after getting the divorce, practically going down on my knees for it, we can't delay the announcement for much longer. I know how absolutely awful it will be for Grace and those two *lovely* children but we have our own lives to think about, and I *have* sacrificed my marriage." She gave a funny little laugh. "I do admit it wasn't the most successful marriage in the world, angel, but then nor is yours, and whatever else, we mustn't be hypocritical, must we?" When he didn't answer she rushed on as if to fill a gap which might prove awkward. "I'm sorry to be so adamant when you had such a bad accident, but — "

She stopped, for a shadow appeared at the table; the shadow of the head waiter who stood at hovering distance, ready to come forward the moment he was noticed. Now he approached with a bow, and a spread of hands.

"I am most vexed to interrupt you. But there is a gentleman downstairs who has been waiting for some time, and who refuses to wait any longer." He added, with the lowered voice of discretion: "It is a Detective Sergeant Golightly, sir. From New Scotland Yard."

5

A Detective Asks Questions

SUDDENLY DOREEN'S HAND was on the back of Hugh's. It was small, slender, beautifully manicured. It was also icy cold.

Her voice was sharp, but there was agitation in it.

"What on earth can he want?"

"I'll go and find out, you go home," said Hugh. He glanced up at the waiter enquiringly. "He didn't ask for Mrs. — ?"

He did not know Doreen's other name. He simply had no idea. It could be anything from Smith to Cholmondeley. And this time there could be no rescue, for why should anyone think there was the slightest need for rescue.

"He asked only for you, sir."

Had the waiter noticed that pause; had Doreen? Or were they both too preoccupied by their own situations, Doreen with anxiety which she could not fail to show, the head waiter for the good name of the restaurant.

"If it would help we will gladly take the lady out by the side door, sir, and send for a taxi."

"Yes," Doreen said, "I think that would be a good idea. Neil darling, I don't know why, but my nerves are so badly shaken today. It must be the shock of seeing you with a police— of seeing you obviously not well. And don't let that other matter worry you too much, sweet, we can talk about it later. Do let me know what this man with the ridiculous name says, won't you. What was the man's name?"

"Golightly, Madame. Detective Sergeant Golightly."

There was, about the head waiter, as there was about most of his kind, an indescribable mystique. He waited just long enough for Doreen to kiss Hugh lightly on the cheek and then he spirited the French waiter out of the air, and said: *"La petite porte. Taxi."* And suddenly Doreen was walking away from Hugh with a lilting movement that was quite new to him.

She really had the most superb legs. When Hugh looked away from her he found the head waiter's eyes on his, and for a moment their gaze locked. Then the man inclined his head and murmured:

"Detective Sergeant Golightly is waiting in one of the private rooms, which is not in use today."

"Good for Golightly," Hugh said, lightly. "I suppose you couldn't give me the slightest indication of what he wants."

"No, sir." A flicker of a different expression crossed the man's face as he said softly: "I was once in the Metropolitan Police Force, sir. I resigned to better myself and I have been very fortunate — which is beside the point. Mr. Golightly is *alone*, sir. That means that whatever questions he asks and your answers cannot be used in evidence — two officers must be present before that becomes possible. Hope that information will prove of some value, sir."

"I haven't any doubt that it will," Hugh said. "Will you answer me a question?"

"If I can, sir."

"How long have I been coming here with my guest of today?"

Astonishment came and went quickly on the other's face.

"At least two years, sir. And about — well, about once a week, I suppose."

"I knew it was a long time," Hugh said, sighing, and then he smiled and went on with obvious admiration in his voice. "And in all that time you have never allowed yourself to find out her name."

"Her — *name*, sir?"

"I had heard of the discretion of such professionals as you, but — "

"I know her *name*, sir."

"And you've never once let on."

"It — it would be unforgivable." The man took out a snow-white handkerchief and mopped a forehead that was beaded with sweat. "To divulge the name of a client whom I've known for *years*, sir, and who often comes with — "

He stopped, abruptly. Across his face there passed an expression which surely suggested that he did believe he had committed — or at least had been about to commit — one of the gravest breaches of professional etiquette and discretion. His mouth opened again and he gulped, but slowly there was a change in him and a kind of cunning appeared: he was wondering whether this strange client had in fact noticed the slip: *that Doreen came here often with other men.*

It was time to stop, Hugh decided.

It was true that he had hoped to find out Doreen's other name, but it would be foolish, perhaps dangerous, to push the waiter too far. And at that moment a man stepped out of a door on the right which was marked 'Picaresque'. He was a brisk-moving, stocky young man in the middle twenties, fresh-skinned, blue-eyed, square-jawed; his sandy-coloured hair grew straight up not only from his forehead, but from all over his head.

There was a frosty glint in his blue eyes as he looked first at the waiter and then at Hugh.

"I must say you've taken your time," he said curtly.

Hugh was much less surprised by what he said than by the obvious fact that a boy like this should be, as he obviously was, a detective sergeant in the Metropolitan Police Force.

"I am sorry, sir." The waiter's voice had returned to its professional suavity. "Mr. Powell injured his arm, as you may know, and it needed some attention. Otherwise he would have been with you ten minutes ago." What a smooth and practised liar, and what an invaluable man to have on one's side!

"I see." Golightly looked straight at Hugh. "You are Mr. Neil Powell?"

The question came right out of the blue, and created a new, quite different crisis. It was not particularly important to deceive the head waiter, office workers, even close friends of the real Neil Powell: all that had been part of a strange, monstrous game which he had been forced to play and had played with vigour and enjoyment. But lying to a police officer in the course of his duty — that was a different matter indeed. He had a moment of panic, and then he smiled pleasantly, and countered:

"Supposing you tell me what you want to see me about, before we go into personal details, Mr. Golightly."

Golightly turned, pushed the door open, and stood aside for Hugh to enter. He said brusquely to the head waiter: "Thank you. Try to make sure we are not disturbed, will you?"

"Most certainly. And telephone calls?"

"Put calls for either of us through, please."

"It shall be done, sir." He inclined his head and walked off as Golightly came into the room called 'Picaresque', which was a room of studied charm, its decor in shades of blue and pink, with here and there a splash of black. A table which would seat at least eight, stood in the middle of the room.

Golightly was smiling faintly.

"Very high-class rogues," he said. "I suppose they gambled here in private groups when gambling was illegal." He led the way to a couple of easy chairs, and in the same moment put a hand to his pocket and proffered his card; it showed him as Detective Sergeant Ian Golightly of the Criminal Investigation Department of the Metropolitan Police and was signed by the Commissioner. "*Are* you Mr. Neil Powell, sir?" he asked.

"No," answered Hugh, flatly, and won an expression of astonishment and an exclamation: "You're *not*?" from this young man. "Not unless I am a modern and somewhat freely adapted version of Rip Van Winkle."

Golightly was quiet for at least a moment before he said: "Then who are you, sir?"

"Hugh James Buckingham, of 12 Cheyne Terrace, Chelsea," Hugh answered.

"Can you show any evidence to prove that, sir?"

"I should have all the evidence — " He broke off, moved his hand away from his wallet pocket, and said; "No."

"You do appreciate that your answers are puzzling, sir, don't you?"

"Yes," agreed Hugh. "You must be nearly as puzzled as I."

After another long pause, Golightly asked in his friendliest tone yet: "Would you care to tell me how things seem to you, sir? There's no need to go into details, but you *are* known at the restaurant as Neil Powell, and under that name have been coming here for years. Moreover, the lady who was with you was heard to address you as Neil."

Hugh sat very still.

The young man's eyes stared directly at him, but no one could now say that they were frosty or hostile: they were curious, the announcement of his real name had certainly shaken him.

"Mr. Golightly," Hugh said at last, "I would like to make a telephone call."

"In my hearing, sir?"

"If you wish. But I should say that I am not going to call my solicitor." Hugh leaned forward and lifted the telephone which stood on a small table between the two armchairs. Immediately an operator answered, and he said: "Will you get me Scotland Yard, please — the new building." Now, Golightly's mouth dropped open in astonishment. "Thank you." There was only a moment's pause before a woman responded briskly: "Scotland Yard". "I would like to speak to the immediate superior of a Detective Sergeant Ian Golightly, please," he said, calmly.

The questions he was about to ask were virtually answered by Golightly himself, for a glance towards him showed him to be not only amused, but entirely at ease. The pause was longer than Hugh had expected, but at last a man spoke in a deep and pleasing voice.

"I'm not sure I'm the man you want, but I may be able to help. My name is Hardy — Superintendent John Hardy. And you are — "

"There seems to be a little doubt about that," replied Hugh, "and it's puzzling a Detective Sergeant Golightly. He is sitting opposite me and obviously amused, but — well, in my mind there is some doubt about *his* identity."

"Really? Has he shown a card?"

"Photo-copies are fairly easily obtainable these days, Superintendent."

"Super—" Golightly began, and he sat up, the smile wiped from his face. Someone pushed a trolley of crockery past the door, otherwise there would have been no sound but their breathing in the room, as the man Hardy responded:

"They are identifiable, but I take your point. Suppose you describe this man to me — will that satisfy you?"

"Completely — if you confirm the description," Hugh answered. "He is about five feet nine inches tall, broad, has a fair complexion, blue eyes, fair hair which stands on end, and a basically Western Scottish accent slightly overtoned by Cockney."

Golightly had raised both hands above his head in a token of mock surrender. Hardy was silent for perhaps twenty seconds before he spoke with a chuckle in his voice:

"You really should be a detective, sir. *Are* you one by any chance?"

"No," Hugh answered. "Neither professional nor private." The laughter was strong in his voice. "May I ask you for some professional advice?"

"Certainly — go ahead."

"I have a very strange story to tell. Few policemen, unless trained in psychiatry, would be likely to believe it. I really don't want to tell the story twice, so should I tell Sergeant Golightly, or may I call my own doctor, or is there some police consultant who might be the right man to listen to me?" When Hardy didn't answer at once he went on with a frustrated laugh: "I really am baffled, Superintendent. If the facts are what they seem to be I went to bed last night as one man and woke this morning as another."

Golightly was now leaning forward, his interest keenly aroused.

"In the same place?" he asked.

"What in the same place — oh. No. Quite different. I am a bachelor. I awoke a married man."

An exclamation, quickly smothered, came from Golightly.

"And I *think* I'm sane," Hugh went on. "Baffled and bewildered certainly — but moderately sane. I now find myself with not only a wife, but a mistress, and there is a third woman who worships the ground this man — who is not me — walks on. All of them appear to accept me as my not-me image. So do dozens of people at the place where I don't work and where I went this morning for the first time. And all of this," he added with deep feeling, "is the truth, the whole truth and nothing but the truth. I swear it."

There was another very long pause before Hardy said quietly:

"Unless you're suffering from some strange form of amnesia, I am as puzzled as you are. But I'm quite sure you're telling the truth as you see it." He paused again and added: "I do know a man who will be fascinated by this story. He is a police consultant in psychiatric matters but not averse to opposing us if he thinks we're wrong. Have you ever heard of a Dr. Emmanuel Cellini, Mr. —" He broke off, then continued smoothly: "Have you ever heard of Dr. Emmanuel Cellini?"

It was Hugh's turn to pause.

The pause was a long one but the man at the other end of the line waited, as Hugh cast his mind back to the many times he had heard of Dr. Emmanuel Cellini, who, in certain *causes célèbres* in the English courts, had performed some remarkable feats with the English law. It was said that at least once he had persuaded a jury to find a young man not guilty of the murder of his mother, and the judge to agree, although kill her he assuredly had. Most of the people in England, if one could rely on the newspapers and the public opinion polls, had believed Cellini to be right.

At last, Hardy said quietly: "I presume you have heard of Dr. Cellini."

"Yes," answered Hugh, now without hesitation. "I have followed most of his cases. Tell me, Superintendent, isn't his speciality the seeking out of devils? Doesn't he believe in what he calls —" Hugh hesitated, only half-remembering the phrase, and was glad when Hardy supplied it for him.

"Genetic evil."

"That's the phrase. Doesn't he believe that in some cases there is genetic evil — an evil born in a man or woman which cannot be changed or taken away. Not original sin exactly, but inborn, ineradicable evil?"

"That description would please Manny Cellini very much," Hardy said. "Will you see him?"

"Yes," answered Hugh, slowly. "Yes. I've never wanted to believe in this theory, but I've always had a horrid feeling that he's right."

"Are you free this evening?" enquired Hardy.

"Yes."

"Then I shall try to arrange for you and Dr. Cellini to have dinner together."

It was only when he had replaced the receiver that it dawned on Hugh Buckingham that *he* was free, but what about Neil Powell?

And what about — Grace?

6

The Helpful Police Detective

"MR POWELL," GOLIGHTLY said, and then, as with apology: "I think I should continue using that name for the time being."

"Whichever comes easier," Hugh made himself say.

Golightly was startled into a laugh.

"I must say I enjoy your sense of humour, sir. I hope I won't trespass on it too far."

"Try," suggested Hugh.

"May I ask you a few questions about what happened in the Strand? That was really why I came to see you," he went on. "A report was made by one of our officers which it was felt should be investigated. If you would be good enough — "

"Golightly," Hugh interrupted. "Will you do something for me?"

Guardedly, Golightly replied: "If I can, sir."

"Talk as if you were among friends."

The young police sergeant stared — and then broke into a chuckle, attempted to smooth down hair which would not be smoothed down, and leaned back in his chair, less discontented now than when he had first realised that Hugh had been talking to a superintendent.

"Am I talking as if I'm in the box?" he asked. "Sorry. I'll try — but I *am* a copper, sir!"

"The questions," Hugh said.

"I'll give you the main one straight. Did you accidentally fall against that bus, or were you pushed?" Now Golightly was every inch the policeman and a man of action; Hugh had an odd, intruding thought: That he would go a long way in the Force.

"I think I was pushed," he answered.

"Can't you be sure, sir?"

"Not absolutely. The pavement was very crowded, some people were pushing past all the time, and I was preoccupied — I was coming to meet Mrs. — er — my luncheon guest whom I'd never seen before."

"And she accepted you as Powell, sir?"

"She behaved as if she did."

"Well I'm — well, never mind, I understand why you were preoccupied! But you think you were pushed."

"Yes."

"What kind of a push?"

"Almost a pale imitation of a shoulder-charge in soccer," Hugh tried to explain. "Someone was by my side, but then someone always was, and then I felt as if he leaned heavily — no, pushed sideways, shoulder to elbow kind of push. And there was a bus just a foot or so from the kerb and a lot of traffic. I can tell you, I was scared."

"I'll bet you were! What did you do?"

"Shoulder-charged that damned bus," Hugh replied. "It seemed my only chance; if I'd fallen between the bus and the kerb I'd have been a goner all right. Mind you, half of this may be hindsight. All I really know is that I met the side of that bus with my right arm, shoulder to elbow. Someone grabbed me — two people, in fact, a man and a girl — and saved me from falling."

"Did you get the man's name?"

"I didn't even get a good look at him, or the girl. They vanished."

"Did you talk to anyone else who saw what happened?"

"Not to say talked. Your policeman said more than most people. Was he the chap who told you I'd been pushed?"

"No," answered Golightly. "It was a passenger on the front seat of the top deck of the bus behind you, and all he told us was that the man was middle-aged, and wearing a bowler — and seemed to charge into you in exactly the way you've described. We have his name and address and we'll be talking to him later." Golightly hitched himself up in his chair, and then asked with great precision: "Are you aware of anyone who would wish to kill you?"

Hugh said with a slight smile: "As Hugh James Buckingham, none at all. As Neil Powell I have no recollection." Then suddenly there wasn't anything remotely funny about it at all, and he asked sharply: "Do you think someone is trying to kill him and he knows and has put me in — "

He broke off, throwing up his hands.

"It's utterly impossible! The whole thing is."

Golightly said with an attempt at heartiness: "Well, sir! If you'll give me your address I'll take you there, and see if you need any more help with that injured arm. Is it hurting very much?"

"It's beginning to ache like hell," said Hugh. He was still very sombre as he went on: "By all means come to my home and check that it exists. I told you the address once. I'll be disappointed with you as a policeman if you haven't remembered it by the time we get downstairs." He picked up the telephone and asked the girl who answered: "Is the head waiter in his office, please?"

"No, sair," replied a girl in broken English. "He go 'ome in ze afternoon."

"I'll call him again," said Hugh, and rang off.

A few minutes later they stepped towards a taxi which was outside the restaurant. Without a smile Golightly gave the direction:

"Number 12, Cheyne Terrace, Chelsea," and stood aside for Hugh to get in. Hugh sat as far as possible without moving. The slightest jolt was now beginning to jar the bruises on his shoulder, and once when the driver jammed on the brakes he winced as he was thrown forward.

But they reached Cheyne Terrace, close to the river and nearly opposite Battersea Park, without trouble; it was twenty-five minutes past four. Golightly asked no questions as they went in the old-fashioned, open trellis lift, but on the landing outside the third-floor flat in the narrow Victorian building, he stopped abruptly.

"Have you a key to this flat?"

Hugh shrugged.

"I doubt it." He took out his key ring — *Powell's* key ring — and tried each of the three Yales on it, unsuccessfully. They stood looking at each other for a few seconds, Hugh wondering how he could possibly convince the other man that he did indeed live here. There was a small brass nameplate on the side of the door: *Hugh James Buckingham.* There was a pint of milk and a small carton of cream by the doormat, but —

Suddenly, Hugh spun round. On the wall close to the lift was a bell push above which was the word: *Service.* He placed his finger on the bell, and then stood listening to his heart thumping, wondering what was going through Golightly's mind. Before long there was a chink of sound which he knew meant that the lift was coming up, carrying, please God, the ex-petty officer who now acted as caretaker and maintenance man at the five flats in the building. Soon, the top of the lift appeared, covered with dust and oil, two cigarette packets, a dozen or so cigarette stubs and some spent matches. The lift crawled higher, and an elderly, gentle-looking man stepped out. Hugh almost screamed within himself as he willed this man to utter his name. For a few nightmare seconds he imagined the other opening his lips and saying:

"Good afternoon, Mr. Powell."

But what he did say, was:

"Good afternoon, Mr. Buckingham. Forgotten your keys again?"

Golightly said, smiling: "I'm sure it will work out, sir. And if you care to give me the prescription that nurse made out I'll see you get some salve for your arm."

The arm, bared as Hugh stood in trousers and singlet, was already badly swollen. Hugh felt a sense almost of collapse, the fear that he would be called again by the wrong name had been so great.

"If you would, I'd be grateful," he said. "Leave it by the front door, will you? I'd like to take it easy for a couple of hours."

"I can't say I blame you. I'll leave a note about your appointment with Dr. Cellini with it."

"You're very good," Hugh said.

"Sure you're all right?"

"I just need to relax."

He needed, in fact, to be alone. He emptied his pockets and put everything on the dressing-table in a room overlooking the river, then lowered himself on the bed with great care, adjusting the pillows with his left hand without difficulty.

He closed his eyes.

Grace.

He could think of nothing, and of no one, else.

He saw none other. Not Doreen, nor Sylvia, nor any of the girls at the office; not Golightly or the three waiters from three nations; not the policeman. As he dozed, or thought he dozed, all he saw was Grace. When he opened his eyes and saw the familiar tall windows, curtains, furniture, of his bedroom he did not see any of them. He saw only Grace. Smiling, frowning, dancing, teasing, sleeping Grace.

A bell was ringing. He knew it had been ringing for a long time and he wished that it would stop. It hurt his arm. Ridiculous. How could any kind of bell hurt his arm? But there it was, playing up and down his arm from shoulder to elbow. It rang and rang and rang until a little segment of his mind opened and he realised that it was a telephone bell. He leaned over to get at it and all the devils of hell ran screaming through his shoulder. He eased himself up to a sitting position from which he could take the receiver with his left hand, and grunted:

"Hallo."

Would somebody call him Powell?

"Mr. Buckingham?"

"Yes," Buckingham agreed. "Who are you?"

"Golightly. Detective Sergeant — "

"I've remembered," Hugh interrupted.

"Mr. Buckingham, I rang to make sure you will be in time. It's already a quarter to seven and Mr. Hardy will call for you at a quarter past to take you to Dr. Cellini. I thought I'd better make sure — "

"Good of you," Hugh replied. "But don't worry, I shall make it."

"Do you need any help, sir?"

"No," Hugh said. "I'll manage." He was already feeling much more himself and went on with deep sincerity in his voice: "I'm more grateful than I can say."

An embarrassed cough came over the line.

"Then goodbye, sir — and I hope the evening goes well."

He rang off as Hugh enquired of the four walls: "Why shouldn't it go well?" Why — Good Lord! He was going to be interrogated by the master of interrogators, a man said to have the greatest reputation in England for judging whether a man was sane or mad; good or bad.

Was there — was there even the slightest possibility that he was schizophrenic? If there were not some doubt, would a superintendent at Scotland Yard have suggested that he should be interviewed by such a man? And unless he rated it of the highest importance would that superintendent be coming, in person, to pick him up and deliver him to the legendary Dr. Cellini?

7

Dr. Emmanuel Cellini

EMMANUEL CELLINI WAS feeling anything but legendary.

In the first place, he had lost a case to the prosecution. A man had been found guilty and fully responsible for his actions when Cellini had been sure that, within the meaning of the law's definition of insanity — or responsibility for one's actions — the man was not. The crime committed had been particularly savage and brutal. Cellini was as nearly sure as a man could be that the newspaper and daily television details before the arrest had greatly prejudiced the jury, although he had to admit that the judge had done little to help.

Judge Mandolini was also of Italian extraction, which added poignancy to Cellini's failure. He was also a judge with a known predilection for helping the mentally weak and those whose sanity was in doubt. He even worked on a committee, of which Cellini was also a member, whose aim was to make the laws on insanity more humane, and at the same time make control of those found guilty but insane stricter than it was at present. Had Cellini been able to choose his judge for that particular case it would have been Mandolini, and he had lost. A man he believed not to be responsible for his actions, a man he believed should be under the strictest medical supervision and control — and surveillance for that matter — was at the beginning of a twelve years' prison sentence.

Here then was a strong reason for Cellini being dissatisfied with himself. It was not the failure that rankled . . .

"Manny, you senile old idiot," he said aloud in interruption of his thoughts, "of course failure in a trial rankles. It always has, it always will."

So, he was honest with himself, and at the same time explained the second reason why he was not pleased with himself and far, far from legendary. For his wife, Felisa, was away. She was not staying at some English resort for a week or two, ready, almost any day, to come back to him. She was in Italy for *two months*, the first of which was not yet gone, visiting hosts of relatives as far apart as Venice, Turin, Rome, Naples and even Sicily.

It was not that he envied her . . .

"You miserable old hypocrite," he growled aloud, "of course you envy her. And now you have failed in a case which made you stay behind and you have another, coming soon, which you can also lose. Admit it! You should retire."

At that stage he had gone to his one solace: food.

Felisa was a quite magnificent cook, but even she admitted that there was some quality about his chicken cacciatore which eluded her. Perfect! Superb! And he enjoyed making the sauce and pottering about the kitchen. So there were some compensations.

"Perhaps," he complained to himself about the time that Hugh Buckingham and a bus were in broadside-on collision, "this is the way I will go down to fame. *Chicken Cacciatore Cellini*." After all, he had a famous name: why not use it. The thought put him in a better humour, and he gave way to an impulse, one he had quite frequently, and went into the room overlooking the heath where he lived. In here was a glass cabinet with four golden caskets, each casket wrought by Benvenuto Cellini, said to be one of his forbears. By chance, sunlight from the window of another apartment was striking these caskets, and it was as if the gold had caught fire.

It seemed a sacrilege that he did not go down on his knees and worship them.

He examined the three smallest ones first — small only by comparative standards, for the fourth was larger than the rest. These, he had inherited. They had been in his family for generations. For these, he and Felisa had risked their lives, smuggling them across the Austrian border at the end of the regime by the midget Dolfuss and the beginning of the regime of the obscene giant, Hitler.

He nodded and his lips moved as if in prayer.

Next, he turned to the largest casket: a gift. A magnificent gift from a couple he had been called on to help, and had helped, and who lived happily together in a house that was like a museum — and who had thought of the perfect way of saying 'thank you' for our lives, our future together, our sanity. At least he had helped some. Conceited old has-been, of course he had been right, ten times to one he had been right.

He —

What was the matter with him? It was nothing to do with being right: anybody given the training and the experience could be right about an issue, but *proving* that to the satisfaction of a court and so freeing a man or woman, that was not so simple. Being right was easy, winning a case for another as he had for these two who had never even gone into a police court, that was different. And face the truth. He *was* a conceited man. Before he took a case he considered its worth in his time and the person involved: conceit number 1. Having taken the case, he then worked on it until he had probed to the very truth. Number 2. Having established the truth to his own satisfaction he had to convince others. Failure to do so hurt, and could barely be tolerated.

He was just about to unlock the showcase and touch the cherished caskets when the telephone bell rang. There was an extension in this room and a little resentfully he contemplated it, for although no bell in the house was strident, this one had disturbed a reverie and a pleasant anticipation. Then a golden thought entered his mind: it could be from Felisa! He sprang to the telephone and snatched up the receiver.

"This is Dr. Cellini."

"Hallo, Manny," said a familiar voice, "I hope I didn't disturb your post-prandial."

"How often have I to tell you, John, that in the first place I do not sleep after lunch, and that in the second, a post-prandial is after dinner?" But the severity in his voice was due to his disappointment. If it could not be Felisa, however, then the next best was John Hardy — the man he most liked and respected of all his friends.

"As you say," said Hardy unrepentantly. "But Manny — have you some spare time, preferably this evening?"

"I have a chicken cacciatore being prepared, and if you would care to come and join me I would be happy."

"Don't tempt me. I am ringing about a rather mysterious case. I want you to see the young man involved, and the meeting would be better without me. If you could have him to dinner it would give you plenty of time to form an opinion of him."

"A preliminary opinion, perhaps."

"An opinion strong enough to advise me what I should do."

"Hmm. Somewhat of a responsibility," exclaimed Cellini happily. "Then, if I am to advise, yes, I certainly will give this young man dinner. Even his appreciation of the food will be some indication of his character. But John — "

"Yes."

"Can you not bring him here yourself, and have a drink with us, so that neither he nor I will feel strange?"

"Splendid idea," approved Hardy. "What time will be best for you?"

"Well, now — as I am cooking myself — shall we make it a little late? Say, seven forty-five here. That will also give me time for a bath and even what is, I believe, called 'forty winks'. Seven forty-five here would suit me admirably."

"I'd forgotten Felisa was away or I would have — " Hardy broke off, and chuckled before he went on: "That young man doesn't know what a meal he's going to get! By the way, 'young' is comparative. He is in the late thirties or early forties."

"To be that age would make me feel I had the secret of eternal youth," declared Cellini. "I shall look forward to seeing you and the not-so-young man very much."

He rang off, then moved slowly towards the four caskets. But in the few minutes that his back had been turned a change had come over them. The sun had moved, and only the handle of one casket was still afire. Disappointed, he moved on to the kitchen. The chicken, boned and yet replaced so that it looked whole, was already soaking in a sauce of which only he and Felisa had the secret; but there were a few tiny additions to be made. Busying himself happily with these, he basted the chicken reverently, and then took out a packet of green and a packet of white spaghetti, weighed these in his hands and finally put the green one away. From the bottom of the larder he took some fresh leaf spinach, very young, and washed each leaf before putting it in a colander.

Now he was free for an hour and a half. So he went to his study, a small, book-lined room, adorned with a bust of Socrates and another of Plato, and sinking into his favourite armchair fell immediately asleep. There was no miracle involved in waking; an alarm clock would go off at six o'clock and he could not be late.

His last reflection was on John Hardy.

John would not have asked him to see this man unless he had a very strong reason indeed, and few people had a keener nose for possible deviations from the psychic norm than John. This time, however, he had been remarkably reticent — not even giving the man's name, or a hint of the trouble involved. In other words he wanted him, Manny Cellini, to have a completely unprejudiced mind about his visitor.

Cunning old John!

Before sleep captured him, Cellini smiled; he was happy again. Hardy's request had, for a while at least, wiped out the memory of that defeat.

The front door bell at Hugh Buckingham's flat rang at ten minutes past seven. This would be Hardy, of course. He wondered what he would make of him, whether he would prove to be as pleasant as he had sounded.

A big man stood in the hall. Broad-shouldered, well-covered, his silvery-grey eyes only a shade or so darker than his hair. He could have posed as everyone's family physician.

"Superintendent Hardy?"

"Yes. Good evening, Mr. Buckingham."

"Will you come in for a moment? I'm practically ready."

"And I'm a few minutes early, traffic was very light tonight," said Hardy, stepping inside. As the door closed behind him they looked at each other in mutual appraisal. Then Hugh spoke:

"Will you have a drink?"

"Thank you, but I don't think so, as I'm driving."

"The policeman who practises what he preaches! Not a sherry? That can't harm you."

"The man who sold the idea that the alcohol in sherry isn't as potent as any other alcohol was the best public relations officer the liquor business ever had," remarked Hardy. He followed Buckingham into a large room, neither immaculate nor particularly untidy, with bookshelves on either side of a fireplace, a few sporting prints, and what looked like some genuine Max Beerbohm sketches. There was an imposing row of Charles Dickens, in what was a very early if not an original edition. The Persian carpet was wearing in patches by door and fireplace.

"All I need now is a handkerchief," explained Buckingham, "and I always keep them here — it exasperates me when I have to go right back into my bedroom to get one!" He opened and shut a drawer in a deep chest. "I'm ready."

Hardy stepped out, following him to the sound of the lift gates clanging one or two floors below.

"If that's going down we might as well use the stairs," suggested Hugh. "It can take forever." He watched the cable which controlled the lift cage and said: "No, it's stopped, so unless some benighted tenant has left the gate unfastened, we should get it at once." He pressed the bell, and immediately the cable moved, the great weight passed them as the car came up.

Hugh followed habit and looked down, always wanting it to come faster than it did.

Hardy also followed habit, and looked about him — and saw a man standing in the doorway of the flat opposite Hugh's. Suddenly he roared "*Look out!*" and thrust Hugh to one side.

Hugh, above the agony of his bruised arm, felt fear, for crouching low, with a stocking pulled over his face so that he would be impossible to recognise, was a man with a gun.

Two shots flashed; cracked; struck the doorway of Hugh's flat. One could not have failed to kill him had he been standing waiting for the lift.

"Drop down!" Hardy roared.

Vaguely, Hugh was aware of the gun being turned towards him, and sight of the muzzle pointing towards his breast broke through the pain again, and he flung himself downwards. He did not see the flash but he heard the sound, then heard Hardy shouting, a clatter of noise, another shot, the ping of a bullet on the metal sides of the cage, footsteps thudding down the stairs, the whine of the lift — and then silence.

He stirred, and got on to one knee. He could hardly believe that a bruised arm could hurt so much, even now it felt as if someone was battering on it with a flat piece of wood. But there was no near sound, except what was in his head, and at last he opened his eyes. If Hardy had gone down in the lift to try to reach the bottom floor before their assailant he might be shot as he stepped out, might be killed.

But there *was* Hardy! He was lying in front of the closed lift gates.

8

Man Alive

OH, MY GOD, thought Hugh: oh, my God.

He put his good arm against the wall and then eased himself into a position to get up, watching Hardy all the time. The man did not appear to move. There were no sounds from below and no one appeared to have been disturbed. He reached his feet and stepped towards the man on the floor — and then saw Hardy's eyes flicker and his mouth move.

He was alive.

Hugh reached him as his eyes opened wide. Hardy looked at him; at first vaguely, and then with dawning recognition.

"So you're all right?" he muttered.

"Yes, I — but what about you?"

"Slipped and banged my head," Hardy said, ruefully. "That man wasn't such a good shot. Lend me a hand, will you?" Hugh put down his left hand and Hardy hauled himself to his feet. "Thanks," he said. "Don't you have neighbours?"

"Only deaf neighbours, apparently."

"None so deaf," Hardy growled. He hesitated, and then said : "I'd like to go back to your flat and use the telephone."

"Of course. And anything I can get you — "

"Yes," Hardy said with a smile, "a cup of tea!" They

went back into the flat and Hardy sat in Hugh's big leather armchair with the telephone near it, while Hugh went to put a kettle on. He was only just beginning to realise how near death had been: *he* could do with a drink! He poured a little brandy from a small decanter he kept there, and heard Hardy saying:

"I want a driver *quickly*. And I want a full murder investigation team at 12, Cheyne Terrace, Chelsea ... No, no murder but two attempts and I was nearly one of the victims ... Better send Division but tell Division to call on us for anything ... I'll give you the full story as I'm on the road ... What? ... No, I cannot wait, that would mean keeping Dr. Cellini waiting ..." He chuckled, and then added: "Get a car here quickly — both a patrol car and that driver."

He rang off, as Hugh went into the room, carrying tea, milk and sugar on a tray. His eyes lit up.

"Just what I needed," he said. "I'm going to have a bruise as big as a hen's egg on my head and I have a feeling that if I drink even a spot of anything stronger I'll lose what little equilibrium has been left me. Did you hear the instructions I gave?"

"Yes," Hugh answered. "Are you sure you're wise to come?"

"Yes," answered Hardy, and he paused long enough to pour out a strong cup of tea. He lifted it to his lips. "Yes, because I can do no more here than anyone else — I can describe the man and what he wore but I can use the radio for that as we go. And I want to tell you one or two things about Dr. Cellini on the way." He drank more tea, and was about to speak again when there was a ring at the front door bell. Hugh went to open it. Two policemen and a man in plainclothes stood there.

"Driver for Mr. Hardy," this last man said.

"Is the Superintendent in here?" asked one of the policemen.

"Yes," Hardy called. "May they come in, Mr. Buckingham?" He met them in the hall, took a set of keys from his pocket and handed them to the man in plainclothes. "The car's parked about fifty yards along, to the right of the main door. Bring it up, will you? We're going out to Dr. Cellini's."

"Very good, sir."

"I'd like you two to stay here until the team arrives from Division," Hardy went on to the others. "If any residents or anyone else comes, don't let them touch a thing — if anyone goes towards that front door" — he pointed to the place where the man had hidden — "don't let them. Be very nice to them and promise they won't be kept long."

"Right, sir."

The second policeman said diffidently: "Sir, what about the lift?"

"Well, what about the lift?"

"Would it be a good idea if someone stood by it downstairs, sir — and stopped them from smearing any prints?" He was so nervous that he could hardly get the words out.

Hardy studied him for what must have seemed an agonisingly long time, before he said:

"Yes. You go down and do that. We really need someone at each floor for each entrance. Call another of your patrol cars, will you, and fix it."

The man's eyes were bright with gratification and pleasure.

"Oh, yes, sir! At once, sir. Thank you very much, sir." He hurried off, already tugging at his walkie-talkie, while Hardy gave a little smile, turned to Hugh, and remarked: "Amazing how you can overlook the obvious."

"You *did* have that blow on the head," Hugh said, "and — " He broke off, suddenly overwhelmed by the

fact that only five — ten? — minutes ago Hardy had
saved his life and he had not only failed to say 'thanks'
but had actually not given it a thought. He felt the
blood rushing to his cheeks as he looked at the
policeman, and then said in a tone of great humility:
"And if it hadn't been for you, I would have been shot
and almost certainly killed. Mr. Hardy, I — I — I can't
even begin — "

"Don't try, Mr. Powell," Hardy said, without a change
of expression.

"Mr. Powell."

There was a trick question if ever there was one:
timed perfectly, when he was most off balance and his
nerves taut and strained to their limit. He felt a flush of
anger but must not show it. This man was only doing his
job, and already he knew that he was very good at it.

And — he was suspicious.

He considered the dual-personality possible.

That must be why he wanted Dr. Cellini to see him,
Hugh Buckingham. Was he one person? Or was he two?

Even the thought was madness; but not in the eyes
of this man or of Dr. Cellini.

"Sooner or later I shall have to try," Hugh said. "I'm
sure that in the same circumstances Mr. Powell would
have to, too. Have you any idea who shot at — us?"

"You," Hardy said. "I was only there by chance."

"And you don't have any idea who it was?"

"No," said Hardy. "No." He walked slowly towards
the door. "Leave this front door unlocked, constable,
and then get out on to the landing." As the man hurried
off, he said thoughtfully to Hugh: "The chap who
thought of the lift will make a detective one day." He
felt his head and then lowered it to Hugh's startled gaze.
"Would you mind seeing if there's any bleeding. If there

is perhaps I ought to have it washed and an antiseptic put on."

It really was the most beautiful silky, silvery hair, rather darker at very close quarters than it appeared from a few feet away.

"There," Hardy said, and placed a forefinger gingerly on a spot. With equal care Hugh parted the hair, saw a discoloration and a swelling but nothing else.

"No blood," he said, "but why not have a dab of the lotion I was told to use for my arm?"

"Can't do any harm," Hardy conceded.

As soon as Hugh had applied the lotion they went downstairs. Already men were on duty at the lift doors. An elderly man and a youngish woman were arguing at not being allowed to use it. Hardy led Hugh past this. The car, a large, old-fashioned Austin, was double-parked outside the entrance, and almost as soon as Hugh had settled in, Hardy was talking on the radio telephone, reporting what had happened. The part which most astonished Hugh was his description of their assailant.

"The man was five feet six or seven in height, thin, with a narrow and concave chest. The whole of his face was hidden by a woman's nylon stocking which flattened his features, though the prominence of the nose suggested it was abnormally large and possibly hooked. The face was thin, the chin long and pointed. He wore a lightweight suit of greeny-blue. The lapels were narrow. The shoulders sloped, the left shoulder noticeably more than the right. He wore no waistcoat. The trousers had been newly-pressed. His shoes were of suède with rubber soles, a pale brown with overlays at the instep, cut in a saw-edge pattern. He used his right hand with which to shoot. I am not positive but he seemed to tread more heavily on the left foot and leg than on the right, which, together with the additional slope on the left shoulder, might mean a limp — quite

possibly permanent." Hardy paused for a moment and
then added: "He had a broad tie, patterned but with
the same basic colour as his shoes. I saw neither tie-pin,
tie clip nor cuff-links." He paused and then leaned back
and said as if with a sigh of relief: "I think that's the
lot."

The man from *Information* at Scotland Yard said:
"Thank you, sir. I had that sent out on teleprint as
it was recorded — with luck we'll have that chap before
nightfall." ·

"I'll want somebody's neck if we haven't," Hardy
said; and rang off.

He closed his eyes for a few minutes and Hugh sat
watching him. He was pale, not simply from the effort
but from the blow and, no doubt, from shock. But the
description of their assailant had been masterly: there
wasn't another word for it. Gradually, his attention
wandered from Hardy and he wondered how far it was
to Dr. Cellini's, even whether there could be any kind
of surprise packet waiting for him there. If someone had
known Hardy was coming to see him —

Nonsense! The man with the gun had simply been
lurking there waiting for him, Hugh Buckingham, to
come out. Who could conceivably want to kill him? He
stared straight ahead through the late evening traffic,
pondering, baffled and, if he were frank with himself,
more than a little scared. After a while he had a sense
of being watched, and turning, saw that Hardy was
looking at him.

"Scared?" he asked.

"Somewhat," admitted Hugh, without hesitation.

"I had men posted at Dr. Cellini's, after the apparent
attack in Fleet Street, so I shouldn't worry about that."

"Thanks," Hugh said fervently. "Why didn't you — "
He broke off.

"Why didn't I have someone at your flat?"

"Yes."

"I understood from Detective Sergeant Golightly that you did not intend to leave until I arrived, and his telephone call confirmed that. I'd had two men across Cheyne Terrace, to follow you if you left alone, and I thought my being with you when you left for Dr. Cellini should be a pretty safe arrangement."

"And my God it was," Hugh said.

"I wasn't half ready," Hardy said, and added with a wry smile: "I shall deal with myself later. I'd little enough time to brief you about Manny Cellini. You seemed fairly familiar with him already."

"As a seeker out of genetic evil — yes."

"Do you believe in genetic evil?"

Hugh said bluntly: "That some men are evil — bad — and beyond redemption?"

"Yes."

"I think there may be such a pathological condition, but until we've learned as much about the brain as we have about the body, we can do nothing about it."

"Hmmm," mused Hardy. "I should like to be with you and Manny tonight, but I can't be. I want him to meet you without any foreknowledge of the case, and without any sense that what he says and asks, and what you say and answer, can, be inhibited. He had no idea who you were — *either of you!* — what has happened, what you think or what you want to do. I asked him to see you as a friend — of mine, I mean — and if he thinks there is any reason to suggest that he should act for you then of course he cannot also act for the police. I hope I've made myself clear."

Hugh said slowly: "I heard what you said, I'm not sure that I understand it, but that can wait. What I want to ask you is this: why are you taking this trouble over me? I'm an ordinary citizen who may — "

"No, Mr. Buckingham, that's not true. Any citizen who has been within an ace of murder twice in one day is extraordinary." Hardy rubbed his chin and then, very gingerly, touched the bump on his head. "If you really don't know why — apart from the attacks on you — you are of interest to the police, then I'd rather you stayed in that state of ignorance until you see Manny Cellini. After he has questioned you for a while and you've told him what I've said to you *he* may realise why I — why we, the police, are so interested. And he'll tell you. If he doesn't tell you tonight, I promise that I will tell you tomorrow morning. Does that make the mystery easier to bear?"

Hugh's doubtful expression changed to a smile.

"A little."

Ten minutes later they reached the London outer suburbs where Cellini lived, and in fifteen minutes they were standing on Cellini's doorstep.

9

'Old' Man and 'Young'

HUGH BUCKINGHAM'S FIRST impression of the man who opened the door was of a small, old, apple-cheeked man. His cheeks were of the purest pink, his hair incredibly white. The parting of a perfectly trimmed moustache was meticulous.

The wide-set blue eyes beneath bushy white eyebrows were questing; friendly, but questing.

His voice was gentle, yet had the precision of a foreigner. There was nothing odd about his voice or his handshake.

"John, it is good to see you." Obviously his grip was firm; nothing significant in that; but his gaze was penetrating. "You have a bad headache?"

"I'll tell you about it later," Hardy said. "I would like you to meet Mr. Hugh Buckingham."

His shake *was* firm; but there was gentleness in it, and the moment when Hugh thought the nerve pains would shoot to the upper part of his arm, faded at once. The old man, who was rapidly getting younger every minute, stood aside for them to pass, directing them, with an almost imperceptible nod to Hardy, to a room on the left. The evening sun was shining straight on to those incomparable caskets, afire again as if they would blaze through the whole room. Cellini had taken them out of their cabinet, and they now stood on a Genoese silver table.

Buckingham stood absolutely still; he hardly seemed to be breathing.

Cellini said in a gentle faraway voice as if he was an oracle from some distant land :

"Can a man who is in love with beauty be wholly evil?"

Hugh heard the words but did not at once understand their significance; he was too dazzled, too bemused. He drew nearer the caskets, making no attempt to touch them, as he examined each one.

At last, he finished, and turned to Cellini.

"I hadn't realised how illustrious your ancestry was, sir. I feel humbled."

Cellini bowed, a glint in his eyes.

"And can the humble ever be possessed by the Devil?"

Hardy opened his lips as if to protest, but no sound came, for Cellini rested a hand on his arm and said:

"I am not truly being rude, John — I am trying an experiment. And it is your own fault, you know."

"*My* fault!" gasped Hardy.

"Entirely your fault," Cellini insisted, that wicked gleam still in his eyes. "If you had not introduced Mr. Neil Powell to me as Mr. Hugh Buckingham, do you think that I would have been so perverse? Why *did* you?" Now there was reproach in his voice. "Do you really think so little of me that you attempt to deceive me?"

Hugh had seen Hardy in action with his men; some of whom had been in awe, all of whom held him in deep respect. And he had seen him in action, moving with a speed that undoubtedly saved his own life. He had listened to his shrewd questions and admired his quick, alert mind; but it had never occurred to him that any man could treat him, even temporarily, as an erring child.

But that was exactly how he looked.

His expression was rueful as he threw up his hands. "How did you know?"

"That this is Mr. Powell, not Mr. Buckingham?"

Surely *now* he'll get his revenge, thought Hugh; he won't let even Cellini get away with this.

"Yes," Hardy said simply.

"I saw his picture on television this evening."

"Good lord!" exclaimed Hardy. "Already?"

"I happened to turn on the little set in my bedroom — I slept only a short while — and heard the first edition of the news. Some enterprising television cameraman was nearby, preparing for some shots of a film entourage about to visit the Savoy, I believe, and he saw the incident and took photographs of it."

"Stop!" cried Hardy, headache forgotten. "Did he get a picture of the man who pushed — "

"No," said Cellini, thoughtfully. "But he did get one of Mr. Powell at the moment of impact, and I was quite enthralled that any human being should have such remarkably quick reflexes."

"Did it show the man who stopped me falling sideways again?" asked Hugh eagerly.

"Yes. Him and the young lady."

"Then I'll be able to trace them," Hugh said with genuine pleasure, and he flashed a smile at Hardy. "You may be able to help me, Superintendent."

"Gladly."

"Thank you."

"And so we have established one thing, I imagine," said Cellini. "You brought Mr. Powell here because of the attempt on his life early this afternoon, and it is probable this is not the first attempt. Obviously from the force with which he struck the side of the bus, his arm is badly bruised — I almost forgot that in my

surprise at seeing you, Mr. Powell." Cellini paused and
gave a little, puckish smile. "What I don't understand
is what gave you such a headache, John."

"A bump on my head," said Hardy.

"He — " began Hugh.

"When I struck it against a lift, while falling."

"I see," said Dr. Cellini, but it was evident that he
did not really comprehend at all. How could he even
begin to? Why was Hardy deriving such enjoyment
from misleading or at least toying with him? Perhaps
this was an old game played by friends of a great many
years: a 'silly' game to those who saw them for the first
time, but not silly and not pointless; a part, rather, of the
portion of two lives that were shared.

"Who — er — pushed *you*?" asked Cellini, his face
lighting up.

"I fell," declared Hardy, and suddenly there was a
change in his expression and in the tone of his voice.
The playing was over. "You're right in one way,
Manny. We don't know how many earlier attacks were
made on his life." He glanced at Hugh. "But we do
know that one was made after the bus attempt." With
the same lucidity with which he had described the
assailant to *Information* he now described what had
happened on the landing, making very light of his own
part in it. He touched the tender spot on his head
again, and then asked: "Do you think I might venture
a sherry?"

"I would recommend, at this stage, a Dubonnet or
even a very weak gin and dry Vermouth."

"I'll settle for the Dubonnet," said Hardy.

Cellini moved to an Italian cabinet, and took out
bottles which he set up on a small table nearby.

"What will you have, Mr. Powell?"

When was Hardy going to disabuse him?

"I think I'll have the same," Hugh said. "I'd rather
my blood didn't race too fast this evening."

On that instant he had a recollection of his blood running fast and his heart beating so that it had almost choked him. When Grace had leaned over him in bed that morning. He stared at the portrait of a woman on the wall near the cabinet, of a beautiful woman, with colours which could make it conceivably a Titian, but he did not see the face, he saw Grace. He heard a sound which was a long way off and then recognised it as a man's voice, but it was still too far away for the voice to be distinguishable.

Grace — Powell.

Neil — Powell.

He felt hot. He knew he was sweating. He felt a touch on his arm, and at last the voice and the words penetrated:

"Mr. Powell, will you please look at me."

Grace. The woman of the portrait. Oh, God, he *was* going mad.

"Mr. Powell — look at me."

The voice was louder now, and at last he made himself change the direction of his gaze and look down at Dr. Cellini. The smaller man's eyes were piercing in their intensity and their directness. He stood with a glass in his right hand, while Hardy stayed just within the periphery of Hugh's vision.

"Tell me, please," Cellini said. "What did you see?"

It would choke him to tell of Grace. He did not answer.

"Mr. Powell, I do not know what is happening on this case. I do not know why you are here. I have been asked if I can help you and I will most certainly try, if you will co-operate. But I can do nothing if you refuse to co-operate — nothing at all."

Hugh glanced, again, at the portrait. It was of a red-head, an over-bosomed, beautiful redhead with inviting eyes. Not Grace. Nothing at all like Grace.

Cellini said, quietly: "Would you prefer to talk to me

in confidence? Superintendent Hardy would gladly leave us, to make that possible."

"Of course," Hardy said.

Hugh saw that he looked deeply troubled; not hurt, not rueful, not angry, but deeply troubled. In a different way, so did Cellini. Hugh glanced again at the woman who might have been painted by Titian, and then he forced his stiff lips into a smile and moved his hand for the glass which Cellini was still holding. He would gladly sit down but no chair was near and he did not really trust his legs.

He asked: "What worried you so much?"

Cellini said: "It would be better if you would first tell us, or me — "

"I'll be on my way, Manny," Hardy said, and turned towards the door.

That was the moment when something inside Hugh Buckingham exploded.

"You bloody well stay there!" he roared. He turned furiously to Cellini. "And it wouldn't be better if I told you a damned thing. You've already been made a fool of this evening once *and* by your good friend Hardy, don't stick your neck out again. I want to know from *you*" — he stabbed a finger towards Cellini's chest — "and from *you*" — he jabbed again towards Hardy — "exactly what happened. Why you looked at me as if you were looking at a madman, and then if I can *and* if I think it's worthwhile I'll tell you how *I* felt. Ever since I woke this morning I've been pushed around, made a fool of, twice been nearly murdered, once — oh, to hell with you both. I'm going."

He felt an almost overwhelming temptation to drain the glass and hurl it into the fireplace; he did drain the glass but he restrained himself from throwing it. He did not know what had possessed him to lose his temper as he had done, and he did not care; but by the time he reached the open door he began to understand.

It was because he had recalled Grace so vividly.

But she wasn't there, only a fat old woman tarted up by Titian — or a good imitator of Titian.

The front door was on the right, and closed, of course. He reached out and began to open it. Not once had he looked back and he heard no movement on the thickly carpeted floor. A cool evening wind and a shaft of sunlight came in and at the same moment Cellini called:

"Come back, Mr. Powell, please. I am deeply sorry for any rudeness."

Cellini — apologising to him.

"Come back, Mr. Powell, please." There was a pause, and then: "I know there must be something grievously wrong, and if only because of what happened in my house I would like to try to help."

Hugh stopped moving, but did not close the door. He turned round slowly to see Cellini a yard or two behind him, and Hardy in the doorway of the room from which they had just come.

All anger had gone from him, but some of the causes for it remained.

He said simply: "If I come back, will Mr. Hardy tell you the truth?"

Hardy called: "Yes."

"Mr. Powell," said Cellini, "I do not know what John Hardy has so far withheld from me but I am quite sure that it has been because he believed it the best way to help. Before he does tell me the truth, however, I want to understand what happened to you in this room, just now."

They entered the room again; and the sun had so shifted that the blazing light was gone, only a subdued beauty now remained.

"So as it is what you prefer, I will tell you the truth. You asked both John and me the same question. I cannot answer for him but I will answer for myself. A change came over you as you looked at the portrait.

You looked like — a man possessed. As if a different spirit, almost a different personality were within you. And on your face part of the time there was an expression of great anger and indeed of fury; at others, of rapture, perhaps even of love. I have never seen so many changes in the face of a man in the space of so short a time." He paused, then looked slowly away from Hugh and asked Hardy: "How long was it, John? Four minutes? Perhaps five?"

"I would say five," replied Hardy, huskily.

"And why did I affect you?" demanded Hugh, but there was no emotion in his voice, only a flat enquiry.

"For the same kind of reasons," Hardy answered. "I would add only one thing to all that Manny said."

"And that one thing?"

"I would have said," replied Hardy, "that you were possessed of the Devil."

10

Man Possessed

AFTER HARDY'S WORDS, there was silence, utter silence, as if all of them had been shocked by the words. It did not enter Hugh's head that they were absurd, because he knew that Hardy — hard-bitten, experienced, sophisticated policeman of a lifetime's service in London — believed them. And all this day it had seemed to him as if he were living in the body of another man: or, as if another man were living within him.

Cellini was smiling.

"John, do you remember the first significant question I asked you this evening?" He gave Hardy barely time in which to answer and then gave the answer himself. "And can the humble ever be possessed by the Devil?"

Hardy said: "Yes, I remember."

"It was your second significant question if by 'significant' we mean the same thing," Hugh said. For the first time he felt he had strength enough in his legs to move. He sat down, choosing a chair by the window, facing both men.

"The first?" asked Cellini.

"I remember that, now," put in Hardy. "Can a man who is in love with beauty be wholly evil? There's one thing you omitted."

"I know. The answers. My answer to each question is 'no'. What would your answer be, Mr. Powell?"

"The same as yours," Hugh said, with a wry smile. "But I think you can be pretty bad and still be in love with beautiful things. And I would like to swear any of us know who is humble or why — but need we go on with this. Superintendent — " He broke off, waiting for Hardy to tell the truth about his name.

Cellini proffered a chair to Hardy, while he himself sat down on a tapestry-covered stool which stood close to one of the cabinets. Everything in this room was lovely.

"Thanks," Hardy said, and paused only for a moment before going on: "Manny, I wanted you to find out everything from the man I've introduced as — or rather you presumed to be — Neil Powell. I have good reason for wanting you to find out from him without the slightest prompting from me. I'll explain the reason later — for the nonce, will you believe that?"

"Of course," said Cellini. He turned to Hugh and said simply: "If you are not Neil Powell, then who are you?"

"If my memory hasn't failed me — Hugh James Buckingham," Hugh replied.

"I can vouch for the fact that he has an apartment in Cheyne Terrace, Chelsea, that he is known by people there as Hugh Buckingham, that his name is on the door, that letters all addressed to him are in the apart-ment, that the initials H.J.B. are on the canvas cover of a tennis racquet and on the flyleaf of one of a set of Dickens which I think you'd envy." Hardy paused, turned to Hugh, who was gaping at realisation of how much the other had noticed in a few minutes, and then went on: "The first thing I did *not* want to put into Manny's mind was that you might be a kind of Jekyll and Hyde, or Powell and Buckingham."

"Or a schizophrenic," said Hugh. His throat felt dry.

"Most of us are that, one way or another, some people

live five or six lives and I'm sure that if they could afford
it many men would have five or six wives!" said
Cellini, his expression at its most angelic. "I quite take
your point, John. Now — as so much more has happened than we had bargained for, may I suggest you stay
for dinner. You've no objection, I imagine, Mr.
Buckingham?"

"How could I have? The less mystery there is — "

"Thank you. John — "

"If you are sure there is enough to go round — "
began Hardy.

"Don't be ridiculous," Cellini said. "That's settled
then. And I really should go and dish up — my wife is
away, Mr. Buckingham, but don't be alarmed, I assure
you that the meal will be eatable. If you two would care
to wash while I am in the kitchen . . . John, you use the
main bathroom and show Mr. Buckingham-Powell the
spare room, will you?"

"Of course," Hardy said.

Cellini vanished through a doorway and Hardy led
Hugh along another, wider passage into a pleasant,
rather feminine looking bathroom.

"Whatever we eat will be Italian and superb," he said
comfortably.

"Do you know I've just discovered that I'm hungry,"
Hugh said. "Is there any hurry?"

"He will be at least fifteen minutes. I shall go back
to the casket room."

Hugh nodded, and closed the door — and then could
not resist the temptation of going across to the bed in
the room beyond, kicking off his shoes, and, moving
very cautiously, lying down on his back. It was his
favourite way of complete relaxation; the one thing he
must avoid was dropping off to sleep. He remembered
when he had done so that afternoon, and how the
ringing of the telephone bell had woken him. He *must*

be up in time, for he had a feeling that Cellini would take his Italian cooking very seriously.

What did he really think of Cellini?

Not old, as he had at first thought; for there was an agelessness about him. Wise, certainly, although so far no wiser than other men Hugh had known. Understanding, yes, and in a way compelling: my goodness, he could be a domineering man; far more so than Hardy. Yet this, in fact all of these were simply aspects of his character which Hugh had seen; there was another quality. Gentleness: goodness. Yes, that was it. He was a good man. And after what had just been said it was undoubtedly possible that Hardy had, in a way, brought them together so that he, Cellini, could exorcise the devil in him, Hugh Buckingham.

Lying flat on his back, as physically comfortable as he could be in view of the bruised and now aching arm, he looked at the chandelier in the middle of the ceiling, and said with great clarity:

"What — bloody — nonsense!"

But for his arm he would have jumped off the bed, laughing; instead, he got off cautiously, went to the bathroom and lowered his face for a shuddering moment into cold water. Sobered, he crossed to the bed and smoothed out the bedspread and pillow, worked his feet into his shoes, glad that they were not the tying kind. That done, he went back to the room where they had all met, to find Hardy on the telephone. No one else was there. Hardy beckoned him to stay, showing unmistakable signs of excitement.

Turning back to the telephone, he went on: "Yes, I've got that all right. Keep him at the Yard and let him cool his heels. I don't want anybody else to talk to him until I've seen ... Yes, feed him." Finally he put down the receiver, muttering something suspiciously like: "Damned fools." Then, with a wide grin he looked at Hugh. "I expect you've gathered that we've caught the

man who fired at you. Name of Klebb — K-L-E-B-B —
and he has a record for larceny and one conviction for
robbery with violence. He was caught at London Airport, with a ticket for Frankfurt, had changed his clothes
completely — what do you think gave him away?"

"The limp?"

"Right in one! He'd padded his sloping shoulder but
could do nothing at all about his limp — caused by a
bomb splinter in Malaya, believe it or not. He's at the
airport now, and by the time they run through all the
formalities and get him to the Yard it will be time for
me to leave, and I'll go straight to the Yard to see him."

"Will he say who paid him to shoot me?"

"I doubt it. Unless we can find some kind of
pressure," answered Hardy. "But I've told our chaps I
want to see all the film that was taken of you this
afternoon — it's possible that he was the chap who
pushed you. I — ah! Here comes our host!"

"Gentlemen," said Cellini, from the doorway, "we are
ready. It is my custom," he added to Hugh, "to have a
little Chianti immediately before the chicken cacciatore,
which I serve without any preliminary course; it has
always seemed to me a gourmet's mistake to dull one's
palate with *hors d'oeuvres* of any kind, and to some
degree lessen one's appetite." By now they had reached
a dining-room with a table at which eight could sit in
comfort; he had set the table for three at one end. "I do
not consider it sacrilegious to talk during the meal," he
went on, "and I can hardly wait to hear your story.
But if perhaps for five minutes — " He had them all
sitting, their glasses filled from a Chianti in a basket
container. He then served the chicken from a deep
casserole.

The aroma itself was startlingly good.

The flavour . . .

It was more than ten minutes before Hugh spoke.

"I hope you won't throw me out," he said. "But that

was the second best illusion that I've had today. No food could really be so good."

Emmanuel Cellini beamed at him.

"The flattery of a great lover. Are you a great lover, Mr. Buckingham?"

"Once," Hugh answered. There was no flippancy in the way he spoke, and both the other men looked at him with sudden seriousness. "This morning," he added, harshly.

"To make love superbly, to be saved from death twice, and to have such a meal as this on the same day," said Cellini, who sometimes appeared not to know the meaning of modesty. "You are a lucky man, Mr. Buckingham." He paused, and when Hugh did not go on, he said gently: "We are to hear the whole of your story, aren't we?"

"Yes," Hugh said. "But I doubt if you will believe it."

"You mean, you yourself have doubts?"

Hugh's reply surprised both of his listeners.

"Yes, I have doubts," he said. "And yet I know it all happened. It is as if I have suddenly discovered that I am not one person, but two. I have been trying, when I've had time to think at all, to establish whether I could possibly be *both* Neil Powell and Hugh Buckingham. Once or twice I've almost convinced myself that I could, except for two positive facts. First, Neil Powell goes to an office and is seen by a hundred or so people every day. I do not. I remember what I do with most of my days. The other is that I am not married. However, I woke this morning in Neil Powell's bed, and his wife had no doubt that I was her husband. She seemed a little surprised at my virility, but — " He broke off, spreading his hands. "She was as loving as a happy wife could be."

The others did not break the silence which followed.

He was grateful. There were questions he knew they must want to ask, and many men, on the pretext of seeking the truth, would have asked them. These two watched and waited, and he went on:

"First, I knew I was in a strange place because of the street noises. My bedroom window faces a courtyard; one occasionally hears a cat but very little else. This morning, there were street noises." His voice grew harsh, his breathing laboured. "And — household noises. Someone was having a shower *in* a shower, not in a tub with a curtain, like mine. A vigorous swishing and humming. I couldn't — I simply couldn't believe it." He paused again but neither man, steadfastly watching him, spoke. He could not know that his face was beginning to wear the same look that it had worn during that strange trance of not much more than an hour ago.

He seemed to *see* Grace come into the room.

He drew back in his chair, drawing a hand across his forehead.

"It happened. It was not a dream, unless all this is a dream. She came into the room, wearing a robe as carelessly as if she were alone. It was one of those towelling-robes with huge flowers on it. She was getting some clothes out of a drawer — flimsy things. Then she saw me and for a moment looked quite startled. She was a complete stranger, but — she came to me. She teased me as — as I imagine a wife will tease her husband if they're happy together. And then quite suddenly she wasn't teasing, and I — " He gulped, and moistened his lips before going on: "Well, there it was. In all my life I have known nothing like it. Pleasure yes, but — not this."

He stopped.

And then he said: "She kept on calling me Neil. I knew I should have stopped her, I suppose I don't know to this minute why I didn't, but — she kept on calling me Neil. And I couldn't bring myself to argue or deny, even to think. I suppose if I thought anything, I thought it was a dream. I hated to dispel it. She began to tell me

I would be late, leapt from the bed — but how grace-
fully! — and hurried away to cook bacon and eggs as
if it were the most natural thing in the world. Neil this,
Neil that. I think she was happy — I mean happier than
she usually was. And then — something strange happened. I mean — strange in her! I called her 'sweetheart' and for some reason it subdued her."

"Do you know the reason?" asked Cellini.

"Well, she said I hadn't called her sweetheart for
years. It was almost as if, for the first time, she sensed
something was wrong. But — but it didn't last for long,
and she was looking happy again — even radiant —
when I left. I — I keep seeing her, all day. At unexpected
moments. I saw her in that — Titian in your room, Dr.
Cellini."

"So," said Cellini, softly. "Because of the likeness."

"Good God, no! Because — well, she seemed to take
the place of the woman in the picture. And as I stared
at her I realised I wasn't her husband and that I was
never likely to see her again, and that two attempts had
been made to murder me."

The word hovered in the air but neither of the others
spoke, and at last he went on in an anguished voice:

"I hated everybody and everything that would keep
us apart — I didn't understand, I don't understand, for
all I know I may be a madman, or I may be suffering
from hallucinations, I may even *be* possessed. But I'll
tell you one thing," he went on in a harder voice. "I
may be possessed by the Devil now, but this morning
I was a damned sight nearer heaven than I've ever been
in my life."

11

The Understanding of Dr. Cellini

Dr. Cellini leaned forward and placed his fingers firmly on the back of Hugh's hand. He spoke without a vestige of a smile:

"Already I knew how lucky a man you were; now, you tell us of the sublimation. Now! I can offer some ice cream which can be safely recommended, or some torte, which it is true has been frozen. Alas, there is no other way of bringing it here from Vienna and keeping it, but the cream is fresh English cream and to prepare will take only a moment."

"Sacher torte," decided Hardy.

"And for me," said Hugh, speaking with an effort.

"And I shall put the coffee on to percolate — a Brazilian coffee; we can claim to have had an international meal. Your familiarity with Sacher torte suggests that you travel widely in Europe."

"Yes," Hugh replied. "Everywhere."

"Indeed. When we are under a little less pressure I would like very much to hear about it." As Dr. Cellini talked he was placing the dishes on a tray. He indicated a decanter of red wine by Hugh's side. "I recommend a little," he advised, and went off, bearing the laden tray, with Hardy, carrying odds and ends, following.

Hugh poured out a little of the wine, and sipped. It was fuller and smoother than the Chianti; a perfect preparation for a rich, rare dessert. He leaned back in his chair and marvelled. These two men, especially Cellini, had managed to make him talk more freely than he had intended, and he did not think there was much that they failed to know. He suspected that Cellini understood more, but for the moment that was not very important.

The food, the wine, this wine in particular, made him feel relaxed for the first time since he had woken that morning. Truly relaxed. He could think about Grace without tension and anxiety. Therein lay the wisdom of Hardy's sending him — no, bringing him — here. Had a threesome for dinner been intended all the time? He did not think so; that was the kind of deceit which would not help them, and the sense of goodness he felt in Cellini emanated, in a different way, from Hardy.

Well, he had told them all he could.

Could they tell him anything?

They returned, Cellini carrying the Sacher torte, Hardy a big crock of cream. One mouthful, and two at least of the three of them gave to it a near-reverent attention. But it was over at last, and Cellini insisted on leaving the dining-room table as it was — "A woman will come to clean in the morning, and I shall have breakfast in my room" — and carried the still bubbling coffee-pot into a smaller, friendlier room which had none of the museum-like quality of the one with the caskets. The books, from floor to ceiling, the desk, the comfortable armchairs grouped about a fireplace, made a welcome change.

Cellini, having served coffee and brandy, said abruptly:

"Hugh, I want please to explain one or two things briefly about myself. I do believe in evil. Incarnate evil. Evil which in some cases, comparatively rare but real enough, cannot be eradicated. Many people believe in this in different ways. The Christian and the Jewish doctrines, of course, are of original sin. I do not mean that. Some evil may exist in us all, but I am far from convinced. Some instincts are not always pleasant I admit, most of us are capable of violence, of evil-doing, but I believe this is being bred out of man. And I believe that the incarnate evil is due not to a spiritual but to a material, a physical maladjustment of the body and brain. I do not ask you to believe me: I am simply telling you this so that you can understand what I say and do more easily. I hope that is clear."

"Very clear," answered Hugh.

"To be compelled, as some people are, to be bad, evil, corrupt, beyond redemption is in itself a terrible thing. But I believe far more of us are temporarily possessed — a better word might be obsessed — by evil things, desires, intentions. For there is always a cause, and although it is not always found, a cure."

"And into which category do you place me?" inquired Hugh.

Dr. Cellini frowned and his voice sharpened.

"You should not be flippant over such matters. I have not placed you in either category. It is just conceivable, but I think unlikely, that you are a split-personality, in which one part of you, unknown to the other, might do strange things. I have seen no evidence of this tonight." He looked at Hardy. "You would not wish me to leave Hugh in any doubt, would you?"

"No," Hardy said.

"However, a fourth possibility remains," declared Cellini. "That you might be a law-breaker. A criminal. Deliberately creating two personalities for yourself for reasons of personal gain."

Hardy looked up from his glass and shook his head.

"No," he stated. "When I was talking to the Yard before dinner *that* was established. There is Hugh

Buckingham and there is Neil Powell. They are separate individuals, and we know the fundamentals of both."

Hugh's heart was racing. "You mean I'm under no suspicion of any kind?"

Hardy said carefully: "We can't be absolutely sure that you and Powell don't sometimes change identity."

"But until this morning — " began Hugh, hotly.

"John is talking from the point of view of proof, as evidence, not probability," interrupted Cellini. "After all, there must be some reason to want to kill you. And clearly it could have something to do with your likeness to Neil Powell. So the police must find the motive, and to do this they must explore all possibilities. It will not help if you get hot under the collar every time something is said that you don't like."

Hugh subsided, grunting: "Sorry."

"How would *you* describe your life?" asked Cellini.

Hugh hesitated for a long time and then began to smile, humour sparkling in his eyes.

"Couldn't we have John's description first?"

"If you wish." Cellini also smiled.

Hardy put his brandy down with a certain reluctance, then spoke with the calm, official precision Hugh now expected of him.

"You are aged forty-one," he announced, "you inherited two hundred thousand pounds from your father when you were twenty-two, and have invested this so that you live on the income from one half, and speculate with the other. Your present worth, financially, is about half-a-million pounds but you still live on the income of the first invested one hundred thousand pounds. You live in a pleasant flat, and travel for about six months every year. You were married before your inheritance and with your father's approval, but your wife was killed in a car accident in which you were not involved."

Caroline.

Fragile, beautiful Caroline.

My God! Possessed by — by any man who took her fancy. Driving with one of her lovers she had been killed instantly.

Caroline.

How it had hurt when, after her death, he had learned the truth about her from an over-officious friend who thought it would ease his mind of sorrow if he knew.

Caroline.

He was aware of silence; he was aware of having slipped back into the world of memory. The two men were watching him. And under their intent gaze he lost the vision of Caroline, and closed his eyes.

"Does the memory of your wife's death still hurt so much?" asked Cellini. "Or was she — unfaithful?"

"What the hell makes you ask that?"

"Because there was both love and hatred in your expression, Hugh. How long have you lived alone?"

Hugh said: "Twenty-one years — since my father's death."

"Did the experience with your first wife so hurt you that you did not consider marrying again?"

"In the beginning. And then I began to live to a pattern which I enjoyed. I came to the conclusion that the really expensive and properly trained woman who makes the use of her body her profession, can give all the needed sexual life. If properly controlled, and not over-indulged."

"And this is how you have lived?"

"Yes."

"And so you have an extensive knowledge of these ladies of pleasure?"

Hugh looked at him at first suspiciously and then decided that Cellini meant the phrase literally, and had uttered it without a hint of censure. So he answered:

"Yes."

"In many parts of the world?"

"In several."

"Do you care to be specific?" As he paused, Cellini added: "I believe it might help John, and the police."

"I don't see how it possibly can," declared Hugh, looking at Hardy. It was surprising how easily Hardy faded into the background; perhaps that was part of his training as a policeman. Now, his glass was on a table by his side and he was leaning back in a chair which he filled very comfortably. "Would it?" He found it difficult to address the Superintendent as 'John'.

"Yes," Hardy answered.

"Very well. I have two in London of whom I have become very fond. They are there when I need them, and never obtrusive. Paris, of course. Copenhagen." He smiled with sudden wryness. "I had no luck at all in Moscow or Warsaw, but Vienna and Milan..." He shrugged. "Am I really telling you all this? I think that's all in Europe."

"Dublin?" asked Hardy unexpectedly.

"No," said Hugh. "What made you ask?"

"Curiosity."

"Well, I can't guarantee that I won't forget somewhere! But I think that is all in Europe. In the United States, New York and Beverly Hills. And — Cape Town — " He shrugged again.

"Why do you travel?" asked Hardy. "Is it simply for pleasure?"

"Good lord, no! It's to make money."

"For some people a wholly satisfying reason, but for you — " Cellini, having started to speak, broke off and raised his hands in an apologetic gesture. "It is not that I question your motives or your rights. I need to know all I can about you."

Hugh looked at him for a long time.

The difficulty was to answer in a way that was truthful but did not sound either self-indulgent, or hypocritical. To explain motives, in fact, which he did not fully understand himself. So the silence lengthened, and without seriously breaking it Cellini stood up and poured a little more brandy, then plugged in the coffee-pot.

"My father died of wounds received years before, in World War II," Hugh said at last. "He was a great idealist and a greater patriot. By the time he died he was already beginning to doubt whether what he had fought for was worth fighting for. My mother had been killed in an air raid in London. He died a bitter man."

For a moment Hugh was lost in the past, then he moved impatiently and went on again:

"Well, I decided he was half-right and half-wrong, that values were changing everywhere and that nothing really mattered any more — everyone, even the newly emergent countries and the difficult rebel or revolutionary groups in each were all travelling in different directions, but a few men were all going in the same way: making money." He laughed, not without bitterness. "If I'd worked at it harder I could have made a lot more money, but I liked to mix business with pleasure, travelling by luxury liner, staying at the best hotels. I simply invested small sums in dozens of countries, in the one staple commodity which needed no work, and simply increased in value while it sat there. Even when taxed the taxes were minimal. I didn't even need an agent to look after the investments for me, and with rare exceptions — takeovers by governments for which there was always some compensation — I couldn't lose. Two guesses as to what I dealt in."

"Land," said Hardy succinctly.

"Land," echoed Cellini.

"Land it is, in places where the value was likely to increase — just outside big cities. I bought in tens and occasionally hundreds of acres — oh, and I didn't even need a secretary, my typing could be done by a bureau, and I used a local lawyer for each transaction. I seldom sell land; I lease it. As all my globe-trotting was to see the land I bought, my travelling was tax free." When neither of the others made any immediate comment, he went on: "I'm not particularly proud of it but I have always salved my conscience by telling myself that I've created some invisible investments for Great Britain, the rents come here and I *do* pay tax on them. So — " He finished his brandy, then placed his glass down with extreme gentleness. Next, he leaned back in the comfort of the large armchair. He had a sense that the others would like to compare notes; he also had a feeling that they worked together so often that their reactions and their thoughts were remarkably in tune; there might well be a genuine telepathy between them.

They were looking at each other as if with a silent question. Then Cellini turned back to Hugh and asked with quiet deliberation:

"Mr. Buckingham, are you a spy?"

12

Scene in Fleet Street

THE QUESTION CAME utterly out of the blue, and was the more shattering because he had told them the simple truth. But Cellini was not joking, and, a faint repetition of his question came from Hardy: "Yes, are you?"

Slowly, he relaxed.

"No," he said.

"Not for any foreign interest but for Britain," Cellini suggested.

"I am not a spy."

"Not necessarily in the usual sense of spying for military purposes, but an industrial spy," suggested Hardy.

"I am not a spy of any kind whatsoever," declared Hugh. He smiled drily. "I almost wish I were, then there really would be some point in what has been happening, wouldn't there. Dr. Cellini — "

"Yes?" Cellini was eager.

"May I have some of that excellent Brazilian coffee?"

"Eh? Oh. Oh, of course." Cellini had obviously expected something much less prosaic.

"Mr. Buckingham," Hardy said, "have you really told us everything?"

"Everything I recall, and I doubt whether I've forgotten much." He stretched out his hand for the coffee.

"Thank you — no, no sugar. What put the spy idea into your heads?"

"You are in a perfect position to be one."

"I am just a playboy who dabbles in business and pretends to patriotism."

"You underestimate yourself and are less than fair," said Cellini. "Have you the slightest idea when you were taken to Mr. Powell's house?"

"None."

"Where had you been the previous night?" asked Hardy.

"In my flat, watching television — there was a good historical play on, a repeat of one of the series on Henry the Eighth, a period in history in which I have always been interested."

"And then?"

"I went to bed — around half past eleven, I suppose."

"You couldn't conceivably be mistaken, could you?" asked Hardy.

"No, Superintendent. I could not."

"If you had been out for the evening to one of your friends — "

"I remember the evening perfectly. I even remember thinking as I went to sleep that what Henry did quite a few men would like to do, although, perhaps, not quite so drastically."

"You know what your story implies, don't you?"

"I know what it means if I'm *not* lying to you."

"Hugh," said Hardy, with sudden and unexpected warmth, "I don't think you are lying. I am getting more and more puzzled, but more convinced that you're telling the truth." He rubbed the top of his head, experimentally. "I am easier than most to convince, especially in view of this. What it means is that after you went to bed last night someone came to your flat, drugged you, took you away, put you in Neil Powell's house, presumably undressed you and put you to bed. All of his clothes were there, weren't they?"

"There was one of my suits and a pair of my shoes," Hugh said. "Nothing except my own could have fitted so well."

"But *his* pyjamas."

"I was wearing no pyjamas."

"Ahem," said Cellini. "All of these things must have happened, John — have you had Neil Powell's house watched?"

Why the possibility hadn't occurred to Hugh before he had no idea; but most certainly it hadn't, and he sat up sharply, hanging on to the words of Hardy's answer.

"Yes, of course," Hardy said, in a matter-of-fact way. "Powell didn't go home tonight."

"What?" gasped Hugh.

"He telephoned to say that he had been sent abroad on an urgent assignment — not uncommon in that department," Hardy remarked. What was it called? Hugh teased himself to remember. Something to do with Overseas Trade. "And he isn't sure how long he'll be gone."

Hugh said simply: "Good Lord!"

"Somehow we now have no Neil Powell we can lay our hands on and question," said Cellini.

"There is another unusual thing," remarked Hardy. But this time his matter-of-factness was more obviously put on, and he managed to appear over-casual. Hugh schooled himself to show no reaction, whatever shock news came next. "The two Powell children have gone to spend a few days with their grandparents." Hardy examined the tips of his fingers as if they fascinated him. "So you see, Grace Powell is at home alone."

Hugh found his heart beating wildly. He knew exactly what Hardy had said, but did not take in any possible significance beyond the fact that Grace was at that house, alone. Cellini moved forward quickly and steadied the coffee cup in his hand.

"And you had never seen this woman before?" he asked.

"Never," said Hugh. "None of this makes any sense — does it? Does it to you?" he demanded of Cellini, and then he almost roared at Hardy: *"Does it to you?"*

"No," Hardy answered, "but there must be sense in it. Hugh, think hard and think back: are you absolutely sure there is no reason why anyone should wish to kill you?"

"I can conceive — " began Hugh.

"John," interrupted Cellini, "I think you almost certainly have the wrong end of the stick. Someone is trying to kill Neil Powell. Hugh is being put up as the victim. You can't seriously doubt that, can you?"

Hardy glowered at him, and then slowly shook his head.

"I must need a holiday or a refresher course," he said, gruffly. "Now that you point it out, it's an obvious possibility, but I hadn't thought about it."

Hugh said wonderingly: "You mean that I am to be killed instead of Powell? *Is* it possible?" In the silence that followed, it came to him slowly that it was the only valid reason for any of the things that had happened.

It could even explain — Grace.

There might be no limit to what a wife would do to save her husband.

There was silence among them all, now, as each considered the situation — and the silence was broken not harshly, but quite positively, by the ringing of a bell: a telephone bell. The telephone in this room was on a table by Cellini's side, and his whole face lit up as if in anticipation of sheer delight.

"This is Emmanuel Cellini," he said, smiling as if the others were not there. Almost immediately, however, the smile faded and he held the receiver out towards John Hardy. "For you, John."

As Hardy took the telephone, Hugh thought: Cellini expected it to be his wife.

Hardy was saying: "Good ... When can we see a run through? ... Yes, I don't see why not, I think he'll be glad to come. Hold on." He placed a hand over the receiver and said: "The Independent Television people have the whole of that film available now, and apparently there is a good picture of what actually happened before, as well as after, you hit the bus. If you'll come to their studio they'll give us a run through. You will be able to see if there's anyone you recognise, too."

"I'll gladly go!" exclaimed Hugh, springing up.

"I trust there will be room for me," said Dr. Cellini, with obvious confidence that there would be. "What time will they run the picture through, John?"

"As soon as we get there," Hardy said. "Which should be in a little over half an hour."

Hugh Buckingham sat in a corner of the car which had brought him to Cellini's house. Cellini sat beside him, while John Hardy sat in front, next to the driver. He was, however, talking to Scotland Yard's *Information* room most of the time. There was a touch of rain in the air but little traffic about and the ride was smooth and pleasant. Hugh lived through memories and half-memories of the day, and above them all in vividness was Grace. Next, perhaps, the startling question: "Are you a spy?" Yes; that came before the two attempts to kill him.

He wondered whether he would have been so readily believed had Hardy not been with him the second time.

At last they turned out of the Strand, almost opposite the spot where the bus 'attack' had been made on him, and the car pulled up outside a building in Kingsway. He knew it by its night signs in vivid neon: *I.T.V.*, but had no close knowledge of it. Two plainclothes men were at the door, both acknowledging Hardy. Another was inside. Almost at once the lift doors opened and a businesslike young woman stepped out, saying pleasantly:

"I'm to take you up to the showing-room. This way, Dr. Cellini."

The others, including the plainclothes policeman, followed along a wide passage to a room of pleasant size, a theatre with perhaps a hundred seats.

A young man, manipulating the projector, turned at once, bursting into speech.

"Good evening, gentlemen. I'm the projectionist and by coincidence, I am the photographer, too. I was on the spot and I'd just been told the stars of screen and stage would be late, God bless 'em, so I was looking about for interesting faces. If you don't mind me saying so" — he turned to Hugh — "yours was one. There were one or two others. I'm a reporter more than a camera-man and had an odd feeling that you were being crowded, and I was able to take some pictures — moving pictures — without being noticed. You're about to see what I took. They only last a minute but a minute can be a long time, on camera. And we can go in slow motion, or stop the projector, if it would be helpful. Is everyone clear?"

Hardy and the others gave a kind of combined growl: "Yes. Thanks. All set."

"Lights," called the young man, and the lights were immediately dimmed; now only one or two showed, the plainest being a red sign saying: EXIT. The projector began to whirr and the beam from it shot out. The pictures were in colour, and startlingly good. Hugh had expected them to be blurred and indistinct; as it was, no one who knew him could have the slightest doubt. A bus, vivid red, was just behind him, and people were passing. One man obviously impeded Hugh, although it was impossible to say whether this was deliberate or not. Hugh was pushed — or edged perhaps was a better word — towards the kerb, and so towards the bus.

Suddenly a man appeared at his side, and beyond any doubt at all, shoulder-charged him towards the bus. From that second everything happened at bewildering speed; Hugh could be seen tensing himself for the collision with the bus, then, at the impact, a man grabbed him by the coat, while a girl, a nondescript looking girl, seized his wrist.

But the astounding thing was the man who had pushed him.

It was Pebblewhite, the tyrant at the office.

In a whisper, he said: "I know who pushed me."

"Shall we have it run through again?" called the young man.

"Can you reverse it for a few feet?"

"Yes, hold on." In a second or two the face and figure of the man who had pushed him showed up again with absolute clarity.

"Stop there!" exclaimed Hugh.

The outline was not so precise as in the moving film, but there wasn't the slightest doubt in Hugh's mind of the man's identity.

"Are you still sure who the man is?" asked Hardy.

"I am absolutely positive."

"Then we won't talk about it here," Hardy said, to the manifest disappointment of the young man. "Would you like to see it run through again?"

"I'm absolutely sure that it isn't necessary," Hugh said.

"Then if we can get a copy sent to the Yard very quickly . . ." Hardy began, only to be interrupted by the projectionist.

"One is available for you to take, sir. Other copies can be made available, if you'd like them."

"I think we shall need several," Hardy said, "but I'll

gladly take the one now, and let you know tomorrow how many we will find useful. And very many thanks." There was an echo of thanks from Cellini and Hugh. They came down in the lift in silence, stepping out of the building into a drizzle. Only then did Hardy allow himself to ask:

"Who is he, Hugh? Where have you seen him before?"

"He is Pebblewhite, the boss at Powell's office in the Civil Service," Hugh answered.

"Then if such a man in such a high position is involved, just what is going on?" asked Cellini. "Why should the head of a department such as that want it thought that one of his staff is dead?"

13

Mad Fool of a Driver

SUDDENLY HUGH REMEMBERED the name of the department; could picture it, so hard to read, on the wall of the new building off Whitehall:

Department of Overseas Trade
Special Services

Hardy was asking: "Do you know this man's other name?"

"Yes. Nathaniel. I could take you to his office, without any trouble."

"How many people did you actually see in the office?" asked Hardy, and Hugh was about to answer: "It must have been about a hundred," when he stopped. They were in the car now, heading for New Scotland Yard. "You don't have to count one by one," said Hardy, with an impatient touch in his voice: as if he were getting tired, or else as if the information that the head of a department of the Civil Service was involved, had affected him badly.

"Perhaps he should, John," Cellini said, and Hardy grunted.

"The point is, I daresay I saw a hundred, but they were mostly in the large office and I only saw them as people across a big room. I couldn't recognise many of them again."

"By the same token," Hardy said, a little less gruffly, "they couldn't have got a close look at you. You were quite right: we need to know the people whom you saw face to face, especially those you talked to. Because they ought to have been able to tell any difference between you and Neil Powell."

"Ah," breathed Cellini.

"It isn't difficult," answered Hugh. "There were only a few. Nathaniel Pebblewhite, a man named Thwaites, Arthur Something Thwaites, he — "

Again, he stopped abruptly, and exclaimed: "I wonder why he was late." He paused, then added: "I told you — I was late, and by chance — I thought — met a man who recognised me, and who was from the office. Arthur Something Thwaites. But *was* it by chance, or was he lurking there waiting for me to make sure I got to the office?"

"If you were to be killed, why should they worry about getting you to the office?" asked Hardy, as if he were talking to himself. Before Cellini or Hugh could reply, he answered his own question: "Unless you actually came *from* the office, you wouldn't be established as Powell."

"Precisely."

"Manny," Hardy remarked, "this is a fiendishly clever scheme."

"Fiendish," agreed Cellini.

"Whom else did you meet?"

"There was a girl named Sylvia, rather a pretty girl, early twenties, golden-haired. She actually persuaded me to leave early, saying how groggy I looked, came out with me when I went to lunch, and warned me against giving up Grace for Doreen — "

"The woman with whom you had lunch at Simpsons?" asked Hardy.

"Yes. Sylvia went so far as to say that Doreen would bleed me dry of money and that I would be crazy to divorce Grace. She said *she* loved me too much to allow it to happen without trying to prevent it." He was actually excited at the clarity of the recollection. "I probably spent more time with her than with anyone but Thwaites."

"Who else?" asked Hardy, hopefully.

"I can't be sure who actually took a good close look at me except for one other, a hunchback named Torino. He was at the desk across the aisle from me, and when he realised I was going to leave early he complained that it would mean more work for him. So I asked Thwaites if he would do the work I couldn't stay to do." He saw the picture of Torino with his mournful eyes and long, narrow face turning to look at him in what had seemed surprise and gratitude. "He almost looked puzzled."

"Four people to question then," Hardy said. "Thwaites — Torino — Sylvia and of course Pebblewhite himself, sooner or later. Can you be sure there was no one else?"

"No one who really looked at me closely," answered Hugh, positively.

A knife flashed through his mind.

Grace.

And another flash which did not hurt but made him cry out: "Could Doreen — "

"How long had Powell known Doreen — can you answer that?"

"The man at Simpsons — now *there's* someone else, the head waiter. I asked him if he could remember how long I'd been taking Doreen — my companion — there, and he assured me that I had done so for at least two years. *Once a week* for at least two years. I tried to get her surname from him but he didn't bite. I *did* trap him into admitting that she often went there with other men. And another thing — when she knew a policeman was waiting for me she couldn't get away quickly enough."

"What did you think of this Doreen?" asked Cellini.

"Beautiful," answered Hugh. "As beautiful as anything made of marble."

Cellini gave a little chuckle.

"So. And do you think Sylvia's warning was justified?"

"Absolutely. All Doreen wanted to talk about was getting married, now that she had her divorce. She didn't give Grace — "

He broke off, as he 'saw' the expression on Doreen's face and recalled much more of what had passed between them. They turned into a narrow street where the 'new' New Scotland Yard was housed, and Hardy said to the driver: "We'll sit here for a few minutes." It was hardly an interruption, if anything it helped Hugh with the vividness of his recollections.

Softly, he went on: "She didn't give Grace a thought — not even a formal 'I'm terribly sorry for Grace, of course'. She just concentrated on the divorce and the need to be quick, and she — my God, she was as nervous as hell!"

"Nervous?" Cellini encouraged.

"Yes — nervous. Jittery. Scared stiff — all the lunch time. But she wasn't a fool, and only a fool or somebody acting under stress would have talked like she did about the divorce. Especially knowing I'd just been so badly shaken up. And — my *God*!" he breathed again, "she was surprised to see me. When I first saw her I realised she was taken aback but I put it down to the fact that a young policeman was with me, and she could see I wasn't exactly myself."

He stopped.

He was caught suddenly by a gust of laughter and could not keep it back.

"Not exactly myself!" he roared. "Do you see what I mean? Could anything be funnier?" He tried to keep his left arm still but could not, and the shaking of his

body was beginning to make the bruises hurt, but it was a long time before he controlled the laughter, and even then he gave a sudden chuckle and repeated weakly: "She could *see* that I wasn't exactly myself."

Over this, Hardy remarked in a thoughtful way: "So we've a Doreen Somebody to add to the list. Check with me, Hugh, please: Nathaniel Pebblewhite, Arthur Something Thwaites, Sylvia, last name not known, and interview I'll tell you. In fact if there is anything of Simpsons. Add the head waiter and — "

"Grace," Cellini finished for him, and the name sounded like a prayer.

"Yes," Hugh answered. "It looks as if — "

"Go on," Cellini encouraged.

"It looks as if all of these in some way or other may be involved in having me impersonate Neil Powell, and be murdered in his place."

"Yes," answered Hardy. "That's it — if what you have told us is the truth."

"I think we have enough supporting evidence to say that it is," said Cellini.

"Yes," agreed Hardy,, "I think so." Did he? wondered Hugh, or was he simply being reassuring for the sake of it? "How do you feel about going to your apartment, Hugh? There will be plenty of our people to make sure nothing happens to you."

"The thought of danger doesn't trouble me over-much," Hugh said, adding wryly: "I shan't see assassins at every corner, and guns in every hand. But — " When Hardy simply waited for him to go on, he added: "Isn't there something useful I can do?"

"There is indeed," Hardy said. "Write down as clearly as you can remember all the countries you've been to, all the places in those countries, and by name if you know them and certainly by address, your lady-friends in the various countries, their telephone numbers

— photographs if you have them — brief descriptions if
you have no photographs."

Hugh stared at him, defiance welling up: what had
his paramours to do with Scotland Yard? Something in
Cellini's expression told him; not in Hardy's. This was
his life, remember; his life or death. He must keep,
should keep nothing back.

Yet his answer came stiffly: "I've no photographs but
I have the names and addresses and telephone numbers.
The rest will be easy. I keep a careful record for tax
purposes."

"Good!" exclaimed Hardy. "I knew tax would justify
itself sooner or later. I'll have you driven home and as
soon as there is news about the prisoner I'm going to
interview I'll tell you. In fact if there is anything of
direct interest to you I'll telephone." He hesitated, and
for a moment it seemed to Hugh that he was embarrassed, which must surely be absurd. "There may be
something I shall ask you to do, later. Will you mind
coming out again?"

"Not if it will help," Hugh said quietly.

The driver was already out of the car, opening the
doors for Hardy and Cellini to alight. He glanced
inquiringly at Hugh.

"It is 12, Cheyne Terrace, Chelsea, isn't it?"

"Yes."

"Thank you, sir. I hope I haven't shaken your arm
too much."

"You've been carefulness itself."

"Thank you, sir." The driver started off with even
greater care, going the King's Road and Oakley Street
way to Cheyne Terrace. It was raining much harder
now, the headlights dazzlingly reflected on the wet road.
Few pedestrians were about. They slowed down for
Oakley Street, and as they made the turn a small car
raced along the road towards them. Swinging right, it
cut perilously across their bows, streaking into a line of

traffic. Even the driver turned his head, while Hugh slewed round, sure there would be a crash. By some near miracle the little car whipped between two others. Headlights shone on the bright red of the vehicle and the head and shoulders hunched over the wheel.

The red car skidded. For a second it looked as if it would crash into a lamp post. Cars on the other side of the road pulled over, instinctively. All waited for the crash to come.

None did.

The red car straightened out and headed for the West End at a wild speed. Hugh's driver shrugged in resignation.

"Lunatic. It was a red Fiat, fairly new, I would say, and the last two numbers on its licence plate were 3 and 6. I'd better call that in I think, sir, he might have been on the run from something." He called the message into *Information*, finished, and then ejaculated: *"What?"*

The single word struck fear into Hugh Buckingham.

And the fear could not have been more justified, for as they turned the corner into Cheyne Terrace a crowd was already gathering about a body lying on the ground.

It was the body of a girl, lying on her back, one arm twisted beneath her. Hugh could have no doubt who she was.

Sylvia.

Sylvia, of the golden hair and gentle face, with blood coming from a wound high on her forehead, dabbling that hair and turning it to crimson.

A patrol policeman said laconically: "She was shot."

"A man was hiding in the bushes, I saw him!" cried an elderly woman trying to hold back an excited terrier on a leash. "I was taking Tiger for his nightly walk and this girl came hurrying along. She looked frightened. And then I saw the man hiding in those bushes." She waved towards the small, crescent-shaped garden in front of the terrace. "He pointed something at her and there were two bangs, I *heard* them!" Her voice rose unsteadily. "And I saw the poor girl fall. I tell you I saw everything!"

"If you could describe the man, madam — " a policeman asked.

"He was small, that's all I could see, he was small and *white*. I saw that, he was white."

Other policemen and an ambulance were arriving, another woman was calling out: "I didn't see the man but I did see the girl fall, and just afterwards a car engine started up very loudly."

"It was a little red Fiat," a man remarked. "I was on the other side of the terrace where it was parked."

A little red Fiat . . . A small man hunched over the wheel of a racing car . . . Two shots . . . Sylvia alive and frightened, hurrying to his, Hugh Buckingham's, address . . . Sylvia, shot dead so that she could not talk to him. What other reason could there be? These thoughts went through Hugh's mind as, for a few moments, he knelt on one knee beside her, and saw a face which seemed, in his distress, much more familiar, yes and much prettier, than it really was.

Hardy's driver was saying: "I think we'd better go upstairs, sir. Mr. Hardy will know about this by now."

Upstairs. Past men at each lift stop. To his flat, with two men at the landing. Inside — the two men going in first to make sure the flat was empty. Then quite suddenly he was alone, the door closed, two men guarding it.

He thought of Sylvia.

He 'saw' Grace.

Oh, God, what would happen to him if he should ever see Grace lying dead? The very thought made him feel he was going mad.

14

Question for Cellini

"WELL," JOHN HARDY asked as he pushed open the door of his office at New Scotland Yard, "what do you really make of Buckingham? And Manny — I know he's a likeable chap, so no hogwash, please."

Cellini, who knew the large, square, barely-furnished office well, crossed to a comfortable armchair and sat in it.

"One aspect of him you know as well as I. He told the truth. I haven't any doubt that he could have withheld some part of it, but I don't think he did. I think he told us everything he knows. He is *not* a spy. There is the very relevant fact that he owns land in many places in which the Department of Overseas Trade is concerned, and little doubt that what has happened is connected with this Special Services branch. To say more would be guesswork. However — "

"There is the man himself," Hardy said. "The mind of the man."

"Can you be more precise?"

"At least twice he has seemed to go into a kind of trance. I have seen epileptics rather like it before having an attack. He isn't normal, Manny — all right, all right," he added hastily. "He doesn't *seem* normal, to me. Why, his attitude, his feelings, his emotional stress even at mention of this Grace whom he has only seen once and who appears to have behaved like a trollop, isn't natural. There is something strange about him."

"John," said Cellini, quietly, "there is always something different, if not actually odd, about a man who chooses to live alone."

Hardy gave a lopsided grin. "Thanks."

"You have very little time in which to be odd," said Cellini, "but when you compare yourself with your fellow superintendents, the married ones, don't you often feel a kind of odd man out?"

Hardy scowled.

"But I do *not* go into trances."

"We don't know that Hugh Buckingham does usually. We know he has apparently settled for a very comfortable life which many a married man would envy. There is the streak of Spartanism, or simplicity — call it what you will — in him which makes him live here in London on a much lower scale than he need. He leads a normal enough sex life — "

"If you ask me, he has a more fulfilled sex life than most married men."

"Perhaps. But this isn't a diatribe on sex, John! I think I know what is the matter with what you might call his mind, but I would rather call his spirit." He helped himself to a drink of water from a carafe on Hardy's desk, and then went on: "He is an extraordinarily lonely man. He shares virtually nothing. It is extremely doubtful whether he ever confides more than trifles to anyone. Lonely, then, and in many ways isolated. What does such a man do, John?"

Hardy answered: "Live in the past."

"With a young, very beautiful, completely amoral wife whom he worshipped and whom he believed to be faithful. No sensitive man could possibly live happily with *that* image. He comes to see women, then, as sex symbols; for him, a pleasant but brief physical activity. He has no one to argue with — so, he always has his

own way. Taken by and large and in those circumstances I think he has turned out remarkably well."

"*If* he's what he says he is."

"Yes, of course. But in my opinion there is one part
of his mind sealed off from the rest, from the world.
What happened this morning broke the seal. And now
this Grace Powell has suddenly become to him what
every man secretly needs: his ideal woman."

Hardy said: "I daresay you're right."

"Breaking a seal which has been fastened for a long
time in a sensitive mind can only cause extreme pain,"
Cellini went on. "He is beginning to live in a new kind
of anguish; I think we saw the birth as distinct from the
conception of it in my apartment this evening."

"You mean, when he was transfixed by the painting
of the woman."

"Ah," murmured Cellini. "Yes, John, and so much
more. The painting is so much more than of a woman.
There was some quality in Titian which enabled him to
capture some aspects of *all* woman: to show in one
face and body what every man can perceive as perfection
of a kind; not a woman, but womankind. Wife, yes;
mistress, yes; and mother, sister, daughter, all these in
one. Hugh Buckingham has lacked all of those, and
suddenly saw them in his Grace this morning, and then
because the same qualities were in the portrait, saw that
woman as Grace. For a long time we have had a man
with a part-damaged mind and spirit but that part
sealed off, buried in the subconscious. Now the wound
is open again. I would not like to say what will happen
to Hugh Buckingham if — " Cellini hesitated, and then
went on: "I would like to say *if*, but I should say *when*
this illusion is shattered."

Hardy said shortly: "As it has to be."

"It will be a miracle if it is not. So, John! You have
your main problem, the police problem, why is the
impersonation being done, who is behind it, how much

more danger will there be? And we share the other problem; what is going to happen to Hugh Buckingham when — "

The telephone bell on Hardy's desk began to ring. Hardy put out his hand but did not lift it, and Cellini finished: " — the whole truth is known."

Cellini stopped. Hardy lifted the telephone, announced: "Hardy," and then lost colour so suddenly that Cellini was not only startled, he was alarmed: for Hardy looked desperately distressed, as if this were news which he could never have believed possible. He said: "How is Buckingham?" and Cellini felt a measure of relief. "Where? . . . Alone? You bloody fools! Open the door and see if he needs anything, talk to him . . . I'll be there in twenty minutes."

He banged down the receiver.

He said in a growling voice: "The girl Sylvia was hurrying to his flat this evening — half an hour ago, and was shot dead. Buckingham arrived a few minutes afterwards — you heard what happened." He lifted the receiver again, and barked into it: "A car, at once, please," and went on to Cellini: "We have a description of the murderer's car, a partial registration number and a vague description of what he looked like. A call's out." Returning to the telephone he asked: "Who's on duty? . . . Yes, of course I mean who's in charge! Put me on to him." He looked at Cellini, eyes turned towards the heavens, and asked: "Am I the fool? Or is everyone else behaving like a moron? . . . Hallo, Luke. Come and see me at once, will you, please? . . . Dr. Cellini is here." He rang off and wrote swiftly on a sheet of paper until the door opened and Superintendent Luke came in. He was a solid man, with a look of imperturbability. "You two know each other, don't you?" Hardy said, and each of the others replied "Yes", without any of the usual courtesies; it was as if they knew that Hardy was concerned only with one

thing: time. "Luke," he went on, "here's the name of a
Government Department and the names of three people
who work there — Pebblewhite, Torino and Thwaites. I
want their homes located, and a full account. Have two
men visit each. If it can be done without arousing the
individuals themselves, that would be fine. But I have
to be *sure*. Got that?"

"Yes," answered Luke.

"Then there's a woman named 'Doreen', according to
our reports recently divorced. We don't know her surname. The head waiter at Simpsons probably knows the
surname — married name, if she was in fact married.
She's a beauty, Spanish type. I want her located and
kept under surveillance too. Get cracking, will you?"

"Right away." The Superintendent nodded to Cellini
and went out. Hardy wiped his forehead, which was
running with sweat, and made a few more notes on a
slip of paper. He stood up.

"John," said Cellini. "Grace."

"Grace's house has been closely watched since it was
known she was alone," John Hardy answered, "and I
made sure it was covered from all sides and from the
rooftop. And that wasn't only for her sake," he added.
They were out of the room and walking along the
passage towards the lift, now.

"I don't think I quite understand you," Cellini said.

"It's for his, too."

"Buckingham's?" Cellini exclaimed.

"Yes," said Hardy. "I think we're going to have to
find out what happens if he goes there again posing as
her husband. Last time he didn't know about it, but
tonight he will." The lift doors opened and as they
stepped inside, he asked: "Do you see any objections?"

"I am by no means sure yet that I see any advan-
tages," answered Cellini, "and I am not sure he will go.
But we can think about it on the way. You are certainly

right about one thing, he should not be allowed to stay
alone. But John — "

"Yes?"

"You are playing tricks with a man's mind."

"Manny," Hardy said, "I have no choice, and you
must realise it."

Cellini did not speak.

A different, younger driver was at the wheel of the
same car when they reached Broadway. The weather
had worsened, and the rain was now teeming down,
splashing up and hissing from the ground and running
down the gutters.

There were fifty or sixty people at Cheyne Terrace,
in spite of the wild weather; among them newspaper-
men and photographers. The body had been removed,
but the ambulance had remained in the roadway, its
doors closed. The divisional man in charge had borrowed
a policeman's waterproof cape and another policeman
came up with one for Hardy. Umbrellas were everywhere. Cellini glanced at Hardy, who nodded and said:
"Send a man up to Mr. Buckingham's room with Dr.
Cellini, will you?" A man standing under the porch of
the house came forward and was told what to do.
Cellini preferred the lift, all doors of which had been
checked for the second time that day.

Two men were on the landing, and another was inside
with Hugh. They were in the inner room, and to Cellini's
surprise they were sitting opposite each other, drinks at
their sides. Although he looked pale, and his eyes
appeared to be brighter than normal, Hugh did not look
as bad as Cellini had expected.

Both men stood up.

"Dr. Cellini, I told you about Detective Sergeant
Golightly, who came to see me at Simpsons." Hugh was
even trying to joke. "He was on special duty here
tonight and volunteered to keep an eye on me, I
imagine — "

"Oh, nonsense," Golightly protested.

Cellini said drily: "Good evening, Sergeant. I'm very glad to find you here."

"I'll be just outside if I'm needed," Golightly said, making one of his futile efforts to smooth down his upstanding hair. "Please let me know if there's anything more you want." He slipped out unobtrusively, as Hugh turned to Cellini.

"Drink?"

"No, thank you. Shocked?"

"No one could be more shocked than I."

"A guard has been put on all the others," Cellini said.

"No one is likely to be hurt unless they're going to tell me something," Hugh said, and the anguish sounded clearly in his voice. "That must have been it, mustn't it. She discovered who I really was, or else thought that I was the real Powell hiding out here, and came to warn me. What other explanation could there be?"

"I think, none," Cellini answered.

"She looked so — so young."

"So I am told."

"For God's sake stop being tactful and non-committal — what are we going to do? Tell me *that*!" cried Hugh. "What is going to happen next, and how can we stop it? That poor kid — "

His telephone bell rang and he looked at it with an expression which amounted to sheer malevolence. Cellini said calmly: "May I?" and lifted the receiver. "This is Mr. Hugh Buckingham's apartment," he announced.

"Thank the lord you're there," said Hardy, in a voice which was surely the voice of doom. "How is he?"

"Fair."

"Manny," Hardy said carefully, and at his precise enunciation Cellini became suddenly, terribly afraid. "I would not have believed it could happen so quickly, but there has been another murder."

Not Grace! Cellini felt like screaming.

"The little hunchbacked man was found dead in his bed with a knife wound," Hardy went on, and the relief Cellini felt, unreasonable though it might be, showed in his face sufficiently to ease the tension in Hugh's, while Hardy went on: "The nightwatchman at the department knew where he lived, that's how we got on to him so quickly, but we haven't yet been able to trace the others. I can tell you one thing, though. Grace Powell is still up — apparently reading — in her front room. Do you think this is the time for Hugh Buckingham to go to see her?"

15

Second Visit

"John," asked Cellini, holding the receiver a little further away from him, "it is clear that others, who knew that Hugh and the man Powell were not one and the same, might be killed, isn't it?"

"I think so," Hardy agreed, and Hugh, seeing Cellini nod, knew what the answer was.

"Including Grace Powell."

"It's obviously — possible." Hardy seemed to have some difficulty in speaking.

"And also including Doreen — do we yet know her name?"

"Wiseman."

"Doreen Wiseman," said Cellini, for Hugh's benefit. "Has she recently been divorced?"

"Yes."

"And do you yet know with whom she has lunched at the restaurant — or other restaurants for that matter?"

"We have two names: each of a wealthy married man."

Hugh breathed close to Cellini's ear: *"We want to know more about Grace."*

"What was that?" Hardy asked sharply, obviously hearing the whispering.

"Hugh, becoming a little impatient," Cellini answered, but he gave Hugh a reassuring smile. "The problem is one I often face with you, John — there appears to be an idea that I have only to be asked a question and I can give the answer forthwith, rather like an ancient oracle. But I really have to think. John — is Hugh under any particular suspicion?"

"Until we've settled this business everyone involved is under suspicion to some degree or other, but — particular suspicion? No, I can't say so."

"You would not object to him going to see Grace Powell?"

Hugh drew in a sharp breath, and moved closer to the telephone.

"To what end, Manny?"

"To find out what he could about her and her husband."

There was a short silence, while Hugh stood with one clenched hand on the table and the other by his side. The room itself was very quiet.

He could 'see' Grace.

He heard Hardy cough, and then say: "You know what he feels about her in that odd way."

Odd be damned! Hugh actually raised his fist as if to thump it on the table, but a movement of Cellini's small pink hand deterred him.

"I also know that it leaves you with some doubt as to whether they really *are* strangers."

"Yes," Hardy admitted. "But at other times I find it impossible not to believe everything Buckingham tells me. Do *you* think it wise to let him go to see Grace Powell?"

"I think it may be the only way of finding out what has really happened," replied Cellini, and now his hand touched Buckingham's in quick restraint. "It will depend on two things, John. First — whether Hugh will go."

At least he realised there was some doubt.

"Second, on her reaction," went on Cellini. "This morning she appeared to take it for granted that Hugh was her husband, but she may have been playing a part in the plot against Hugh. If, in fact, she was deceived, then she is likely to be so again, and she will almost certainly talk to him, as to her husband, about any matter of common interest. He could then bring us a report — he might, for instance, conceal one of those fascinating little tape-recorders in his pocket."

Why the devil should I spy on her?

"If she is playing a part I think he will be sensitive enough to know almost from the beginning," Cellini went on, "and once he was sure of that, he would do everything he possibly could to find out more about her."

"Yes. Yes, I would do that," thought Hugh, and he remembered his *"Why the devil should I spy on her?"* and now he knew the answer. Two people — apart from the attacks on him — murdered in cold blood, including sweet Sylvia: yes, he had to find out, even if it meant lying and cheating and pretending.

There was another pause; not in fact a long one but to Hugh it seemed long, and his nerves were so much on edge that he was at screaming point. Why didn't Hardy make up his mind?

Hardy said: "I think he *should* go — if he will go knowing what he's there for."

"If he goes, he'll remember," Cellini said. "I will talk to him, John." The relief was very clear in his voice; this was the first time that Hugh had realised how much he, Cellini, wanted him to go and see Grace Powell. "Have you any special instructions?"

"Let us know when you start out. I'll want him followed, and want the number of men at Powell's house doubled. I want him to go either in his own car or in a taxi, and — hey, Manny!"

What on earth had got into him now?

"Yes, John," Cellini replied quietly.

"I'd like you away from his flat at least ten, preferably

twenty minutes before he leaves," Hardy said. "That flat may be watched by someone we haven't yet discovered, and I don't want it to look as if you two have hatched up some plot."

He doesn't want to take any chance that Cellini will get hurt, thought Hugh Buckingham, and he warmed to Superintendent John Hardy.

"I shall do just that," promised Cellini.

"Where will you go?" Hardy wanted to know.

"I have a friend with a very comfortable flat not too far away, and he once gave me a key and told me to go there if ever I were stranded in London." Cellini was smiling as he spoke, while suddenly Hardy gave a deep chuckle.

"That's fine," he replied. "I haven't changed the locks."

He rang off.

Hugh, half-amused by the way Cellini had said he would be staying at Hardy's flat, still tense because of what he was to do, moved away from the telephone. Knowing this was no time for long and pregnant pauses, Cellini said briskly:

"Will you go, Hugh?"

Hugh said stiffly: "Yes."

"You heard enough of what John Hardy and I said to know what you have to try to do?"

"Yes," Hugh said brutally. "Find out whether she's fooling me, whether I can fool her, and whether I can learn anything which would help the police to find out what this affair is all about."

"Precisely," Cellini said. He took a small box, pill or snuff box, it might be either, from his pocket, opened it and proffered it to Hugh. Inside were some white tablets. "I would like you to take two of these," he said. "They are sedatives which will steady your nerves and help you to control your reactions, and they will have absolutely no after or side effects at all."

Hugh looked at him steadily, and then slowly shook his head: "I will do what I can as I am."

"They will also kill the pain in your arm," went on Cellini, "and I believe they will help you to do what you most want to do: find out the truth about Grace Powell. I *am* a doctor, Hugh. I do know what we want. I would not be likely to give you anything to impede you. Take them, please — oh, and be sure not to drink alcohol for at least four hours after you have swallowed them."

He obviously took it for granted that Hugh would obey.

Was it imagination or was there some near-hypnotic quality in the man's eyes?

Time was slipping by.

With a sudden movement Hugh picked up two tablets, put them on the palm of his hand, went into the kitchen and took the tablets with a drink of water. Cellini nodded, and moved towards the door.

"My heart and my hopes go with you, Hugh."

Hugh said gruffly: "Thanks."

"I will talk to Hardy on one of the walkie-talkies," Cellini went on. "Will you wait for at least fifteen minutes?"

"Yes," said Hugh, and thought: *It will take me at least ten to shave.*

Fast on the heels of this thought came another: How did Powell get home at nights, especially when so far as the office was concerned he was away on one of his missions? Freshly-shaved? Clean-collared? Or with a scrubby stubble and a grubby collar?

"Has he left?" Hardy asked Cellini, the moment they were through on the walkie-talkie radio.

"No — but I don't think he will be more than another fifteen minutes."

"What mood is he in?" Hardy said sharply.

"I think, a good one. I am sure — "

"Manny, listen to me. I keep seeing him as he was in your apartment, when he looked almost — savage. Supposing he finds out that this woman knows — and *knew* — he wasn't her husband. Will she be safe with him? He looked as if he could kill — "

"Do you mean, is he likely suddenly to see her as the trollop he learned that his wife was, and seeing her so, might attack her because of this subconscious wife hatred he has felt since her death?"

"That's *exactly* what I mean. Rather than risk her life I would stop him from seeing her."

"It will not happen," Cellini declared.

"You can't be sure."

"I am absolutely sure," Cellini replied in a voice which brooked no denial. "I gave him two pills which will keep him calm. He won't necessarily keep his temper, and he might shout and abuse her to some degree, but he will not be violent."

There was first a pause, then a chuckle, and then with both laughter and admiration in his voice, Hardy said:

"You wily old fox. I should have guessed."

"I admit being puzzled that it surprises you," remarked Cellini, somewhat smugly. "I am sure you have guessed the other danger and made the fullest preparations."

"That someone might follow him and kill them both? Or kill her, leaving him holding the baby; or even that she might kill him and swear that it was self-defence? Yes, Manny. No one will get into the house. There is no way of telling whether she will kill him — and if she did and pleaded self-defence I doubt whether the Public Prosecutor would even accept a charge against her."

"It is one of the imponderables," Cellini admitted, "and would clearly depend largely on any evidence that might exist. However, none of these is the possibility which concerns me."

"You mean, there's a fourth?" Hardy's voice held a scoffing note. "I've had two men concentrating on this case and I've given it quite a lot of thought myself, but unless we've missed something so glaringly obvious we just walked past it, I can't believe there is anything. Are you serious?"

Cellini replied in his most gentle manner.

"Certainly I am, John. Have your men searched the Powell house in Chichester Street?"

The immediate response was a sharp intake of breath: and then, quite distinctly, Hardy said to himself: "You blind, bloody fool." It was still some time before he said in direct reply: "No. We have not. We have had no cause to. I can tell you that none of the reports which have come in indicate anyone there but Grace Powell, but clearly there could be someone inside. She went out to a bridge party this afternoon, was back at half-past five, alone. No one followed her, no one has called. But you're still right, a third party might be in that house."

"It looks as if Hugh Buckingham is the one who will find out," said Cellini, slowly. "I wonder whether he should be warned, John. There is still time, if — "

"He left his flat and is driving his own car," Hardy interrupted. "We could stop his car and warn him, you or I could talk to him on a walkie-talkie. But — why the Devil didn't I think of this before? I — hold on, Manny."

Cellini, sitting snug in a police car a few streets away from Cheyne Terrace, Chelsea, nursed the receiver and sat back, glad to relax. He was tired. He was so tired that he was even allowing Hardy to reproach himself for an omission which he, Cellini, should have thought of before. But was it really fair to blame either himself or Hardy? It was doubtful whether the policeman could

have obtained a search-warrant for the Chichester Street
house on the evidence of the attacks on Hugh
Buckingham. After the murders, yes, but there had
hardly been time to think since the murders. No one
could possible be blamed. But if Hugh were warned, it
would not be of such dangerous significance.

"Still there?" It was Hardy, and his tone was
declaration enough that he did not bring good news.
"We're too late — unless he's warned in Chichester
Street. He drove so fast our men lost track of him —
they'd been told not to stop him so they ignored his
speed. He's about due to turn into Chichester Street
now. Any associate of the murderers watching from a
house nearby or anyone in the house would know if he
were stopped. And if he's stopped there, they'll know
the house is being watched. I don't think that's what
we want, is it?"

"No," replied Cellini. "No, John, it isn't. We don't
want there to be the slightest doubt that he's gone to
see her of his own free will."

"We'll have to keep our fingers crossed," Hardy said.
"You go on to my place, Manny, and go to bed. If
there's any news of significance, I'll let you know. I
shan't hesitate to wake you."

"I hardly know whether to pray for a full night's sleep
or not," Cellini said. "Thank you, John."

16

Sleeping Grace

THERE IT WAS — Chichester Street.

He had checked the position on a street map of London — between Arsenal on the north and Petersfield on the south. One or two people were about as he turned the corner. The possibility that he might be followed and attacked again had made him drive at furious speed, but now he had to slow down; he had to know the number.

Twenty-seven: The Gables.

'The Gables' did not seem to be the kind of name that she would choose.

Twenty-one, twenty-three — there it was, Number 27 on the gate post, The Gables in lettering across the top of the gate. There was no light showing from the ground floor, but one shone from the upstairs front room and another from what was probably a landing. The houses along here had roomy garages, which left good space for parking only a few houses along from Number 27. There was no sign of anyone in doorways or gardens; the police were doing a very good job of concealment. He parked the car slowly, more on edge than he would have expected now that he was so close. Then he put his hand into his left-side trouser pocket for his keys. Momentarily he was nonplussed because his own leather case was not there; then he realised that he was carrying Neil Powell's key ring.

He opened the gate of Number 27.

He heard a clock strike — one; he had virtually forgotten time; one hour after midnight.

He walked slowly to the front door, wondering with half his mind which was the key which would open it; with the other half, whether Grace *was* upstairs; and if so, had she fallen asleep? And if she were awake, would he scare her? Questions, questions, questions. Was she expecting *him*, Hugh Buckingham? Or her husband?

Was she alone?

He could not be sure when that question had first entered his head; only at the gate, he thought.

Would he find her alone in bed — or with another man?

God!

He was thinking of her as if she were his wife and owed faithfulness to him.

What business of his was it? If her husband and children were away and she chose to take a lover — what business of his was it?

Remember how his wife had behaved. Be he away for a day or a night — my God, he could never hope to know, *never wanted to know*, how many lovers she had taken. Supposing Grace did the same where Neil was concerned? *What business of his was it?* She was free to live her life as she wanted to.

That morning —

Had she believed him to be her husband?

Or had she, knowing he was not, simply taken a proffered chance with all the promiscuity of —

What business was it of his.

Why was he sweating so? Why were his fingers unsteady as he felt for the keys? Why was he shivering?

The first key he tried would not go in; the second went in but would not turn. It had to be the third, or

else the front door key was not here. It went in. And
turned. Would the front door be bolted? If Grace really
believed that her husband was away would she secure
it in every way possible? He pushed — and the door
yielded. He pushed harder until the door was open wide
enough to convince him that there was no chain. He
stepped inside.

His heart was thumping.

There was a diffused light from the landing, but
although all the downstairs doors in sight were open, no
light came from them. He put the keys back in his
pocket, careful not to make a sound, and at the same
moment realised that Powell, coming in, would not be
so timid. Did Powell whistle? Or sing? Or did he, on
coming home, call upstairs to Grace? He must decide
what to do; must do something.

What he did was the least expected thing. Still moving
very quietly, he went into the front room and found
light from the street to convince him that no one was
there. The dining-room had no light but a glow from
upstairs. He groped for and found the switch. No one
was in here either. He went into two more rooms, one
with a desk and book-lined walls, another with a sewing
machine, an ironing board, a pile of linen and a few
children's toys.

That left only the kitchen and the wash-room beyond.

Both were empty. He checked two doors, one on the
side from the wash-room, one at the back from the
kitchen. They were both bolted and chained, and he
thought he saw a wire which suggested a burglar alarm.

Hardy could not have done better!

A man reported by radio telephone to Hardy:
"Buckingham has looked in each of the downstairs
rooms and seems about to go upstairs. He was not in
any room long enough to do more than check that no
one was there."

"Send the report in writing," ordered Hardy, and as he rang off relief sounded in his voice. But he did not call Cellini.

Upstairs.

This was a reasonably modern house, fifteen or so years old, Hugh judged. He did not think the stairs — carpeted from banisters to wall — would creak, and they did not. Everything was very solid, just as all the furniture was of good quality and expensive.

There were five doors here, one to a bathroom, four to bedrooms — one a girl's, judging from dolls and furry animals, but not a young child's because the books were mainly school stories, and in one corner there was an easel with a shelf of brushes and paints. The boy was of an age for cricket bats and tennis racquets. All this Hugh could see from the landing light.

He opened the door of the next bedroom, obviously the 'spare'. Light reflected from a bathroom mirror through an open door. People *could* hide inside wardrobes. He removed the key from inside the door to the outside, and turned it.

Only the front bedroom with that huge bed remained.

The light from it was brighter than the landing, and as he moved very slowly inside, he saw that it came from a wall-light. He could see the foot of the bed, and a slight hump in the middle.

He thought he could hear breathing.

One person, or two?

What had that to do with him?

It had everything to do with him! For some reason which he did not really understand unless it came from the morning's single act of possession, she belonged to him, as his wife had once belonged to him.

That — whore!

Oh, how he had loved her, how beautiful she had been.

He went farther into the room, his heart beating so

fast that it threatened to choke him. Now he could see all the bed.

Grace.

Alone.

She was lying sideways, away from him.

A book lay open, so near the edge of the bed that if she moved she would be bound to knock it off.

He could hear her breathing; and he could also hear his own, laboured, yet quieting down. The carpet was thick enough for his footsteps to make no sound, and slowly he moved to the foot of the bed, so that he could see her better.

She wore a pale green bedjacket drawn up to her neck; it was cold in the room, which surprised him. Still moving without a sound, he went to the far side of the bed so that he could see her full-face.

Not beautiful?

No, not truly beautiful although so good to look upon. Long, silky brown hair had been tossed back from a face strangely innocent.

The hand over the bedspread was her left hand.

On the third finger was a wedding ring.

She was Neil Powell's.

There was not the slightest reason for thinking of her as 'his'. Was he going mad? What had Cellini said: that he had lived so much in the past that he was sometimes living as much in the past as the present. But he could never, no one could ever, confuse this woman with the other, the one who had once been his and whom he had learned to hate.

Grace stirred. Her hand moved; her head moved; the lights danced in her hair.

He stood staring at her, feeling the sweat roll down his forehead. He did not move. He must not move. He must not go a step towards her.

"Superintendent Hardy?"

"Yes," Hardy said.

"Tolley, from Chichester Street, sir. The man Buckingham has gone upstairs and is in Mrs. Powell's room."

"Are you absolutely sure?"

"Yes, sir," Detective Inspector Tolley said. "I'm in the front room of the house opposite."

"Can you see Buckingham clearly?"

"I've a pair of night glasses, sir, but hardly need them. I saw him come in, and he moved very slowly about the room, with long pauses between movements. Now he is on the left side of the bed from me, sir — the side farther from the landing door and close to the bathroom door. The woman appears to be sleeping."

"*Appears* to be?"

"She was reading in bed, and seemed to drop off to sleep," Tolley reported, "and she's lain absolutely still ever since Buckingham came into the room. He doesn't appear to have disturbed her at all."

"And he's just standing and watching her?"

"Yes, sir. Very tense, I would say. I can only see his profile but I get an impression that he is staring as if in a trance."

"Keep watching, and if he moves towards her before she wakes, break in," ordered Hardy. "I presume you've men in the grounds?"

"Back and front, sir."

Hardy said: "Don't take your eyes off them," and rang off. Seconds later he was listening to the brr-brr of the telephone ringing in his own flat. There was an extension instrument in Cellini's room, surely Cellini wasn't so fast asleep that the bell didn't wake him!

At last the ringing stopped, and Cellini's voice came through. "This is Mr. Hardy's home." Then as Hardy began to speak he went on: "I was in the bathroom, John, I hope I didn't keep you waiting. Is there trouble?"

17

Two Together?

CELLINI PONDERED ON what Hardy had told him for what seemed to be a long time; but Hardy knew him too well to expect a hasty answer.

Then: "You say you have a man watching from the room opposite?"

"Yes."

"And that the blinds of the Powell front bedroom are not drawn."

"Not at the moment, anyhow."

"John, I don't believe the present situation is dangerous, but I do think that outside interference now, from the police or from anyone, could create danger. The pills *will* keep Hugh Buckingham's emotional reactions down to a safe level except possibly the emotion of fear. If he felt threatened then I think he might throw off the control which the drug imposes."

"But you are not sure," Hardy growled.

"Not absolutely sure," Cellini admitted, "but sure enough to make me feel that the risk of leaving them in that room together might safely, and indeed *should*, be taken. But for added security and peace of mind, if your man opposite has some way in which he could cause a distraction should Hugh appear to lose his self-control, it would be good."

"What kind of distraction?"

"Dialling their telephone should be sufficient; or throwing a stone at the window. Anything to create a shock effect and bring him back to the present."

Hardy said, breathing hard: "You really do believe he moves from the present to the past, don't you?"

"Of course," Cellini answered. "We all do — but few of us with such intensity. Some people even glimpse the future. There are minds that have been so affected by shock or tragedy that they live in, and move to and from, different periods of time. Will you have your man prepared to make a distraction?"

"Yes," Hardy promised.

"Bless you, John, you are as remarkable a man as you are a policeman. One other favour."

"What is it?"

"I would like to be in Chichester Street, so that if Hugh needs the kind of help I can give him there need be no delay."

"Go and watch if you feel you should," said Hardy gruffly. "You'll find a man on duty and he'll take you along to the house opposite, the front rooms of which have been put at our disposal."

"I shall go at once!" cried Cellini, with great excitement in his voice.

Hugh Buckingham stood looking down at Grace Powell.

He did not know how long he had been standing there, every nerve tense, nor how long it had been since he had seen the face of his wife, first superimposed upon that of Grace Powell, and then gradually replacing it, so that every little thing about that face *was* his wife's. He was aware of his own tension and his own laboured breathing, and what seemed to be a voice within him, saying:

"You must not go near her. You must not go near her."

From outside, there was the sound of a car passing. Slowly the picture of his wife faded. For a while both faces were merged together and they were like the Titian woman on Cellini's wall. Soon, she faded too.

Despite her stirring, Grace Powell had not woken.

Hugh felt hot and besmirched.

He turned and went into the bathroom, where he had been that morning. Letting the cold water run, he plunged his face into it. Emerging, he felt a different man, not remembering what had happened, only that he had been in the grip of some unbearable tension.

He looked at himself in the mirror. His face was a little pale, perhaps, but on the whole he looked all right. Still careful to make no noise, he went back to the bedroom.

Grace was sitting up, her eyes wide open, her lips parted.

And in her right hand, pointing towards him, was an automatic pistol.

Across the street, the watching detective saw the changing scene, but he did not see the gun: the cause for fear.

Hugh was only a few feet away from the bed and the pistol — so close that if she fired at him she could not miss, but too far away for him to have any hope of knocking the gun out of her hand.

She said sharply: "Don't move."

He did not move as he spoke in turn: "I won't hurt you."

"I'll make sure of that," she said. "And that you won't" — there was a moment's pause, as if something constricted her breathing, before she went on " — rape me again."

"I don't know what you mean," he said.

"You know. It *was* you this morning, wasn't it?"

He could lie, but would there really be any sense in it? In one way the fact that she had discovered that he was not her husband was a relief; he would not have to lie to her again. In another way, the word *rape* cut into his heart. To take a woman against her will: no. But to take a woman pretending to be her husband —

It was madness!

He said: "If I were to try for a week I couldn't explain — "

"You are certainly right about that," she interrupted. "A week or a month. You sneaked in here last night, you got into bed without waking me, and this morning — " She raised her empty hand, tight-clenched. "If you stopped at anything short of that — but to be *used* by a stranger." She broke off and he was sure there were tears in her eyes.

He went a step nearer.

It was not deliberate foolhardiness, it was forgetfulness of the threat, of the fact that she had told him not to go any closer. Before he had finished the one step, she cried:

"Stop there!"

So many questions crowded his mind, perhaps the most important being, why had she failed to 'recognise' him that morning when she was quick enough now? Had she been told by someone else? Had she —

"How often have you taken Neil's place?" she demanded.

So it was a straightforward question: "How often have you taken Neil's place?"

He could tell her the truth but would she believe him?

"And how often have you — used me?" she demanded, as if finishing the sentence for the first time.

In this sense he hated the word 'used' but at least it was better than 'raped'. He gulped, trying to find the right words to speak convincingly. He thought he knew how to begin, and moistened his lips, his whole mouth so dry that they seemed stuck together. He simply could not get out enough words: they would not come. Only the one explosive utterance:

"Never!"

"You are lying to me."

His throat was too dry to cope.

"Can I — " He stopped because his tongue literally clove to the roof of his mouth.

"Can you what?"

He gulped. "A drink. Water." There was a carafe by the side of her bed, with a tumbler capping it. His gaze went towards it for a moment then back to her.

She said: "Come and take the carafe, but don't — don't try to get the gun."

He felt such a fool. He felt such a coward. He was so frightened — but it was not only fear of the gun. It was because there was so much he did not fully understand. He did not doubt that she would let him take the water, nor that she would shoot. He was very close to her. She wore some perfume with which he was unfamiliar, but which he thought he had noticed this morning. He looked away from her to the carafe, picking it up with both hands. Then he backed away — feeling his legs press against a chair.

Slowly he lowered himself into it. He poured out a little water and drank, then drank again.

"Thank you."

"Now tell me the truth," she said.

What good would it do simply to iterate what he had already said? There must be some way to convince her, or at least to start her on the way to believing.

"The truth," he said slowly, "is that I must have been made to — to do what I did this morning. But that doesn't alter the fact that it was the most — most memorable experience of my life. How is it *you* didn't know that I wasn't really Neil?"

She had been about to flash some retort to what he

had first said, but his question threw her off balance, and, frowning, she replied:

"I — I'm very short-sighted, without my lenses."

Lenses? Contact lenses, that explained it. That would explain everything — *everything except his voice.*

He found himself saying: "And you were without your hearing aid as well?"

For a moment he thought he had made a dreadful mistake; the words had come without a thought, and she would probably take it as an insult, or at best think he was trying to make light of something that was vitally serious.

But she didn't raise the gun or shout.

Instead, a change came over her expression and she smiled; and then, as if it burst out of her as his words had from him, she actually laughed. It was a low-pitched chuckle, but it came naturally; unforced. Relief went through him in waves.

"So," she said, "a funny man."

"I'm sorry but — my voice *can't* be like your husband's. Not exactly like." When she didn't answer he asked, his smile vanishing: "Or can it?"

"No," she said.

"So?"

"If you're hinting that I *knew* you were a stranger — "

"I swear I'm not. I'm just wondering how on earth it happened that you didn't know my voice was different from his."

She said stiffly: "And this time *you* may not believe *me.* Neil changes his voice sometimes."

"What?"

"It has something to do with his job, and he practises on me."

"Good God!" gasped Hugh.

"The voice didn't surprise me," she said, "but when you called me 'sweetheart' — " She stopped. "I puzzled about that all day. It was really that which made me begin to wonder. We — we have our moods and our moments, but we are long out of the 'sweethearting' stage. Do you know what I mean?"

He nodded.

"Perhaps you haven't been married for long."

"Not for — over twenty years," he said.

She leaned forward. "You're *not* married?"

He said stiffly: "Not now."

"Oh," she said, as if that information startled her. "From the way you — " She broke off and there was a hint of laughter in her voice, but something — it was impossible to guess what — took the laughter away, and she said in a very different tone of voice: "Why are you impersonating Neil?"

"I am *not*," he replied.

"I've been told your name is Hugh," she said, "and Hugh, I *know* that is a lie. Neil's boss telephoned me late this afternoon and told me that you were impersonating him, that you had actually tried to pass as Neil at the office this morning. And I *know* you impersonated him here last night and this morning, and here you are again tonight. *Don't interrupt.* In fact he told me that Neil wanted me to send the children away, there was a possibility of danger to them. Now, tell me why you're impersonating Neil."

Hugh felt his heart beating very fast as her expression hardened and her grip on the pistol tightened. Again, he wondered how he could convince her by simply repeating his denial; and a question which would at least change the direction of her thoughts came to his mind.

"Save the children, sacrifice the mother. Was that Neil's idea?"

Her eyes flashed with anger.

"You forget — I have a gun. You've no right here. You're a burglar. I've every right to shoot you. Give me one good reason why I shouldn't."

18

One Good Reason?

CELLINI HAD BEEN in the front room of Number 26 for only a few minutes. He could see no sign of Chief Inspector Tolley's men. Tolley himself, moving with cat-like silence, had led Cellini across this dark room and proffered him a pair of 'sun' glasses which actually magnified and made it easy to see into the room across the road.

Cellini's first words were almost trite.

"I cannot understand why the curtains were not drawn or the blinds pulled down, Chief Inspector."

"The Battens — the people who live here — say that Mrs. Powell seldom pulls them. She likes the windows open, and I presume the curtains blow about, or the blinds rattle."

"Well, whatever the reason we can count ourselves fortunate. They seem on good terms, don't they?"

"He's sitting down, so she probably doesn't feel so much on edge. They had a laughing session just now but they've turned serious again. May I hazard a guess, Dr. Cellini?"

"By all means."

"This chap Buckingham is quite the ladies' man, and every now and again he breaks her down. Then for some reason she gets suspicious or worried again. They — *hey*!" Trolley breathed. "Look at that!"

For the woman in bed had suddenly raised her arm higher, and they saw that she was covering Buckingham with a gun.

"Shouldn't we break in, sir?"

"You must decide, but perhaps you should check first with Mr. Hardy," replied Cellini. "My own feeling is that any interruption now, any threat from outside, would be more likely to make her shoot than discourage her. After all, he *is* to all intents and purposes a burglar."

"Yes," agreed Tolley, "but I don't like this at all. The man's gone in at our request, we don't want his head blown off." Speaking, Tolley stared at Cellini who had lowered the glasses from his eyes. There was enough light from the street lamps to show the mute appeal, even the touch of despair, in his expression. "Sorry, sir," Tolley went on gruffly, "I'm going over. We cut an identical set of keys." Tolley jingled them gently. "I'll go in myself, sir. No one will hear *me*." He moved towards the door.

"Chief Inspector, at least permit me — "

"Sorry, sir. I must request you to stay behind." He gave an unexpected grin. "You'll see most of the show and none of the risk, if you ask me."

He disappeared. There was a click as the door closed, followed by a second click which made Cellini move very quickly to the door. He grasped the handle, turned, and pushed: but the door didn't budge.

At first, Cellini could hardly believe it. He went through all the movements again, but the door still did not open. He stood in front of it, overwhelmed by such a flood of anger as he had not felt for years: not since the days when he had been forced to accept the utter futility of fighting back against the Nazis by whom he had been governed.

The anger was such that it seemed to burn through

his veins. To lock him, Emmanuel, in, as if he were a criminal!

To lock him in, as if, once he gave his word that he would not leave, he would attempt to escape.

Slowly, very slowly, the rage faded. He went back to the window. Even then, anger was too great to allow him to realise that in the seconds, perhaps a full minute, while his back had been turned, he might have missed a climax in that room across the street.

But he had not.

Grace Powell still sat with the gun in her hand; Buckingham had put down the carafe and held only the glass. He was no nearer the woman; in fact he seemed to be leaning back, as if he felt a little more relaxed.

Hugh was not more relaxed; he was in turmoil. But he felt sure that if he appeared to relax, and not to be frightened, it would be better for him. He kept going over and over in his mind what they had been saying in the last minute or so. Trite-sounding, pointless things, each one loaded with the menace of tragedy.

"I've every right to shoot you," she had said. "Give me one good reason why I shouldn't."

There must be dozens but at the moment he couldn't think of one.

"Give me one good reason." She had hissed the final word.

"You — you — you would always *feel* guilty of murder even if — "

"For killing a burglar? An impersonator? A rapist?"

Then, his first flash of courage.

"Are you sure it was rape? Or was it seduction by a clever woman who — "

"Don't you dare talk to me like that!" she cried.

He didn't care what she said, or how high her voice rose, he was concerned only with the finger on the trigger of that tiny gun. The knuckles of the other fingers

were white, even a nervous reflex could bring enough
pressure on the trigger to shoot him. He sweated — but
he sat still. *Was* she more relaxed? Perhaps a little, just
a little. He actually eased back in his chair.

"Sorry," he said.

"So I should think."

"I didn't mean — "

"You sounded as if you meant I was a whore."

Hugh's mouth dropped open, and the glass nearly fell
from his hand. He could see from her expression that
she was puzzled and it could only be from the way he
looked. He steadied the glass, and placed it on the floor
by the side of the chair. Then, ignoring the threat of
the gun, he wiped the sweat off his forehead. There, in
the bed, were two faces, blurred, merging; his wife's;
Grace's. He closed his eyes but still saw them. He kept
them closed as he said in a groaning voice: "No. Oh
God, *no.*"

He was aware of movement.

He did not open his eyes, it was as if he dared not.

He was keenly aware of the perfume — and, suddenly, of a cool hand on his forehead. She said: "Rest
there," and there was another rustle of movement and a
moment or two later the sound of running water, which
stopped quickly.

Soon, there was a touch at his forehead again, cool
and comforting; a cloth, damped with cold water. She
sponged for several moments, and then sponged both
his hands, backs, palms; finally she drew away.

He opened his eyes.

She was sitting on the side of the bed, a small bowl
of water in one hand, and a towel draped over her
shoulder. The hated obliteration of his wife's face had
gone, and he saw Grace; only Grace.

"Don't talk unless you want to," she said.

Utter peace touched him. He muttered: "I'm sorry."

"I'm sorry you are so — distressed."

"It's my fault," he said. "You — " He broke off.

Gently, she assured him: "It doesn't matter what you say, I won't take offence. I can see that you're — ill. If you want to tell me anything, tell me."

He said simply: "You won't believe it, but I was *brought* here last night. I didn't know where I was when I woke up." He saw disbelief on her face, but went on: "I knew it was a strange place, from the noises. Then — you. You came in. It was — it was as if I were someone else and we — we belonged. You called me some silly name." It was on the tip of his tongue, but he could not bring it out and soon she said it for him:

"Tizzy."

"That's right — Tizzy."

"It — it's a name I use for Neil, sometimes," she said. "I didn't dream that you weren't Neil."

He said carefully, keeping all feeling out of his voice: "You came over to me. Tantalisingly. But — it seemed like love. Not seduction: love. I — I was once married to a — whore."

"Oh, Hugh," she said. "Poor Hugh."

"I shouldn't have called — "

"It must have seemed as if I behaved like one."

"Do you believe me?"

"Yes," she said, quietly. "Yes, Hugh, I believe you. As you believe me."

"Every word," he said.

There was a period of quiet.

At first, it was the most contented few minutes he could ever recall, it was so good to be here and to believe and be believed. And to see her. For a while he could think of nothing else, but slowly other thoughts obtruded: of Cellini, and Hardy, Sylvia and Torino, all the strange confusion of the day. And thoughts must be drifting from the other, daily world into her mind too, affecting the atmosphere, taking away the contentment.

She frowned, then came across to him, placing her hand on his forehead.

"You're better," she said. "Do you often get these — these spasms?"

"Not — not often. At least — "

"The truth, Hugh," she pleaded. "Only the truth will help either of us."

"I know," he said. How solemn they were; how different. "I was going to say, at least, I don't remember having them often. I — " He broke off. "The *truth*?" he demanded. "You really want it?"

"I must have it," she said, quietly.

"I saw a psychiatrist today. I did not understand this — this dual identity and — and I was attacked and nearly killed." He saw her lips tighten and she nodded as he went on: "Apparently in mistake for your husband. The policeman I saw is a senior officer at Scotland Yard. He took me to see the psychiatrist, who — "

"What is the psychiatrist's name?" she asked.

"Dr. Emmanuel Cellini."

"Oh," she said. "The famous one."

"Yes, although he would be the last to say so." This time when he paused she did not interrupt, so he went on: "Cellini saw me in one of these — trances. When I told him I didn't think I had them often, he said that it was probable they had occurred without my being aware of it."

"What do you see, Hugh?" Grace Powell asked.

"Someone who — who reminds me of my ex-wife. Not in features, not — " He closed his eyes and felt her hands fold over his.

"You loved and hated her so."

He said: "I haven't accepted such a thing as love since she went, until — " He was looking at her. "Until this morning. Here. With you. It was as if I'd been — cleansed. Am I being foolish?"

She shook her head, and there were tears in her eyes. He had a feeling that she was seeing him as though through a mist.

"Grace," he said, "I've no idea what is happening. Have you?"

She shook her head.

"Except that Neil's boss told you I was impersonating Neil, and for their own safety you should send the children to their grandparents."

"Where they were glad to go," she said.

"And this man — what is *his* name?"

"Pebblewhite," she answered. "Nathaniel Pebblewhite." Her voice was husky and she spoke with an effort but she was under control again. And the name she uttered was conclusive proof of the fact that the man she had called 'boss' was in fact the Chief of the Department of Overseas Trade — Special Services.

"He tried to kill me this morning," Hugh said.

"*Pebby* did!" There was incredulity in her voice and her expression.

"There is a photograph which proves it," he said.

"Pebby tried to kill — " She broke off, only to start again. "You mean *he* is behind what is happening?"

"He appears to be," Hugh said.

"But that stiff-necked old — " she began, only to break off, and toss her hands into the air as if she could not really believe any of this. She stood up and went back to the side of the bed, and simply stared at him with a complete lack of comprehension. Suddenly the silence was shattered by the ringing of the telephone bell. Grace swivelled round so that she was within hand's reach of the telephone. She turned towards Hugh as she picked up the receiver, and said:

"This is Grace Powell."

She listened for a moment and then said, as if astonished: "Who? ... What did you say?" Apparently whatever had been said was repeated and this time the colour drained from her cheeks and the only word for the expression in her eyes was dread.

She said in a voice that Hugh could only just hear: "Yes, I understand," and then she replaced the receiver.

She did not change her position.

She did put her hand in the pocket of the bed-jacket, where she kept the pistol.

19

Kill?

HUGH SAT WITHOUT moving. Curiously this new development, the sudden return to menace and danger, did not frighten him as the earlier one had done. He watched her, with an abnormally beating heart, as she drew out the pistol.

He said quietly: "What is it?"

She didn't answer.

"Tell me, Grace," Hugh asked. "What has affected you so?"

She tried to speak but the words would not come.

He changed his question: "Who was it, Grace?"

She said at last, in a voice from which all expression had been drained: "It was — Neil."

So her husband had called her. He wondered if he could ease the situation if he tried to be matter-of-fact. The gun, he noted, was in her hand and her forefinger was in the trigger-loop.

"Does he know I'm here?"

"Oh, yes, he knows."

"I wonder how — "

"It doesn't matter how he found out. All that matters is — my children."

He drew in a sharp breath.

"But they are with — "

"They aren't with Neil's parents," she said. "Pebble-white must have lied — lied to me. Lied about Bruce and Gina. They've been kidnapped."

"Grace, I'm terribly sorry."

"Yes," she said. "You have cause to be."

"It's nothing to do with cause, it's simply feeling. I — " He began to get up. At once she raised the gun, pointing it straight at him.

"Don't move."

He said: "I don't understand."

But he understood enough; envisaging the snapping of her tension and the bullet which could so easily kill him. The expression in her eyes had changed, and now they looked as if horror lived in them. He wanted to get up and go to her but was quite sure that it would be fatal; and there was no point in asking questions because he did not know what questions to ask. The soundlessness everywhere added to the tension.

She said: "Hugh," in a taut voice.

There was no hostility in her; he realised that now. There was danger, but it was not born of hostility. Then — what? Her husband had telephoned to tell her that their children had been kidnapped. What —

A stab of understanding went through him.

He said in as clear and calm a voice as he could: "Yes, Grace?"

"They will be killed — " For a moment she actually closed her eyes, as if unable to go on, and then, starting again, the words came faintly. "They will be killed unless I kill you."

He opened his mouth, but what was there to say? He had no doubt that the ultimatum had been put to her as callously as that: kill Buckingham — or the children will be killed. And her husband, their father, was the messenger they had used.

Now, thought Cellini, there is something wrong, badly

wrong. And after a few seconds he said aloud: "I must get across there." He groped for the telephone, found it, dialled 999 by sense of touch and then waited for the ringing sound to stop.

A male operator answered: "Can I help you?"

"I must speak to Superintendent Hardy, of New Scotland Yard, at once," Cellini said.

"I'll put you through to Scotland Yard, sir."

Tensely he watched the woman in the room opposite. She was too far away for him to lip-read, but there was no question of her earnestness or her menace. The gun was now pointing straight at Buckingham.

Was Chief Inspector Tolley within earshot?

The Yard answered and Cellini asked for Hardy and was told brusquely:

"Hold on."

If Tolley was within earshot, and if the danger seemed acute — and whatever Tolley could hear would make that obvious — would he try to get into the bedroom by stealth, or by sudden attack? If he, Cellini, had the choice, it would be by stealth, for the woman's whole attention was so concentrated that she was not likely to hear other sounds. If he judged Tolley aright, Tolley would use swift aggression: burst a door open, risk the chance of being shot himself.

Would Hardy *never* come?

Hardy said: "Hardy. Who is that?"

"John," Cellini said, "your over-zealous Tolley locked me in the room opposite the house in Chichester Street. I need to go and talk to the couple. There's something wrong, and — "

"You can't help this time, Manny," Hardy said.

"How can you possibly — "

"Her husband telephoned her and told her that the two children have been kidnapped and will be killed unless *she* kills Buckingham." Hardy was obviously sure of his facts. "Tolley is on the landing and relaying

all that's said to officers in the street — it's being sent
to my office on a teletype machine, second by second."
When Cellini did not answer, Hardy went on:
"Buckingham is playing it cool, but there's no doubt
he's in very grave danger."

Cellini said: "Did Powell say why this was happening?"

"I doubt if there was time, they weren't on the telephone for long."

"What will Tolley do?"

"I've sent a message instructing him to wait until he
feels sure she will shoot Buckingham. Then he'll burst
in. The door's ajar."

"John, if I were over there — "

"You couldn't do a thing," Hardy insisted. "You're
hoist with your own petard, Manny. You said there was
no way of being sure how Buckingham would react.
Now, there's no way of being sure how she will. You
don't know her, you can't advise on how to deal with
her. I'm sorry, Manny. And I'm doubly sorry you were
locked in. I told Tolley to look after you but I didn't
expect him to be so drastic. He wanted to make sure you
couldn't get hurt."

"He wanted to make sure — " began Cellini in an
acid voice, but he stopped. He had been about to add
that Tolley wanted to make sure that *he* got the glory,
if glory there was to be, but he couldn't be quite sure
of this, and malice wouldn't help.

"Go on, Manny," Hardy said, rather grimly.

"John," Cellini said, "you're wrong."

"What am I wrong about?"

"I could help with the woman I — "

"Hold it!" Hardy interrupted, "there's another
message coming through. She's speaking again." Cellini
could see her lips moving and marvelled that the words
he could not hear were being relayed so quickly to
Hardy's office. *"Listen to this,"* breathed Hardy, and

began to read from the teletype machine in an unbeliev-
ing voice: "I'm quoting: 'Hugh, what can I do, what
can I do. We may have fallen in love at first sight, it
might be real, it might last but — how could we ever be
happy if they were dead because I wouldn't — ' "

Hardy stopped, but Cellini could hear his breathing.

Very slowly Cellini put down the telephone, and went
closer to the window. Now he could distinguish the dark,
shadowy shapes of men moving. The alarm had been
sounded, but just one shot could kill the man whom he
could hardly see.

Her voice said hopelessly: "How can I sacrifice them,
Hugh?"

For the first time since she had started speaking,
Hugh replied.

"You can't."

"I — know — I — can't."

"Your children must come first and we both know
it," Hugh said. "The quicker it's over — "

She was crying, that much could be seen, tears pour-
ing down her face, her shoulders shaking. "But I don't
want to kill you."

"You don't have any choice. You'll be reunited with
your children and with Neil, in a few months this will
all seem like a nightmare. You don't have any choice,
sweetheart."

"Don't call me that!" she cried.

"No," he said. "I'm sorry. But I'm not trying delaying
tactics, Grace. It is a simple fact that it has to be me or
the children, and you can't sacrifice your children for
a stranger whom you chanced to meet."

"Chanced," she said. "Nothing Old Pebby does is by
chance; and there's not very much chance about the
things Neil does. He — Hugh!"

"Yes, Grace?"

"Why should anyone want you to impersonate — you

know what I mean — take the place of Neil, and then be killed?"

"To save him from being killed, presumably," Hugh managed to say quite calmly.

"To make it seem as if he's dead, when in fact he's alive?" There was light in Grace's eyes as her mind began to work above her emotions. "Why should he want people to think he's dead? Why should he want to disappear? Hugh, I don't understand. I — "

At that moment the telephone bell rang again; and the noise seemed as loud and the effect as startling as it had been before. Grace half-turned her head, then looked back at Hugh. She said, more to herself than Hugh: "They're ringing to find out if I've done it."

He said comfortingly: "I won't attack you, Grace. I know you've got to save the children."

She turned her back on him for a moment and he did not move. The telephone bell kept ringing. She changed the gun from her right hand to her left, and then lifted the telephone, saying:

"This is Grace." Obviously she thought it was Neil, as obviously a second later she knew that it was not. Her voice came, gaspingly: "*Who* did you say? Wait — wait a moment," and lowered the telephone so that it hovered, shaking, in her hand. "It's Dr. Cellini," she said. "He says he's in the house across the road — the Battens' house. He — he wants us both to hear what he says."

Hugh moved stiffly across the room towards her and did what Cellini and Hardy had done earlier in the day — listened to a voice coming out of the same earpiece. Cellini's voice was recognisable, each word carefully enunciated.

"Are you both there?... Good... Mrs. Powell, I want you to understand that it is only a matter of a very short time before the police find out who has kidnapped your children... They already know that your husband's superior, Nathaniel Pebblewhite, is involved . . . He of course does not know that the police know this . . . He wants first to have Hugh Buckingham murdered, presumably so that your husband may disappear . . . Are you both hearing me well?"

"Yes," Grace answered.

"Yes — go on," said Hugh.

"As his earlier efforts to kill Hugh failed, he has had to use you," declared Cellini, "and you cannot have any serious doubt that afterwards he will have you killed, for you would know that it was not your husband, but someone else who was dead. He, having gone as far as this, cannot possibly take the risk that you would talk. So the balance is not that of your children's lives for Hugh Buckingham's, but in exchange for you and Buckingham. The odds are not quite what they seemed, are they?"

"I'd gladly die to save them," Grace said, simply.

"I think — indeed, yes, I believe you would," agreed Cellini. "But take the reasoning, and it is very close reasoning, one step further. Who is to disappear absolutely?"

"My — my husband."

"And who called you to relay this threat to the children?"

"My — my husband," repeated Grace, and suddenly she found herself gripping Hugh's hand, while the pistol slipped to the bed.

"Would *he* consent to the murder of his children?"

"Oh, my God!" gasped Grace. "No! They're the two people he loves, he almost worships them."

"I think you should weigh the facts as known very carefully, Mrs. Powell," Cellini said. "Your husband has no great love for you. You are well aware that except at odd moments of physical need when you try to recapture the early days, it is a dead marriage. Do you think he would greatly care if you were dead?"

She didn't answer, but the grip on Hugh's hand was tighter as Cellini went on:

"He is much more likely to connive at your death, and Buckingham's, than the children's," Cellini said. "I don't think they are in danger at all. But I think you and Hugh Buckingham are. I wonder" — he gave a little chuckling sound before going on — "I wonder if you will let me have a word with Chief Inspector Tolley who, if what I am told is right, is standing just outside your door. Tell him to be very quiet, please." And Cellini rang off.

20

The Man Who Disappeared

GRACE SAID IN a hoarse whisper: "Outside the *door*. A policeman."

Hugh took the gun from the bed and moved silently to the door, Grace following. Nearing it, they heard the sound of subdued whispering.

Hugh pulled the door wide open.

Standing outside was Chief Inspector Tolley, a man completely unknown to him. He was holding a microphone to his lips.

Both were astonished, but Hugh spoke first.

"Can you *prove* you're a policeman?"

"I — ah — yes, I — "

"Whisper!"

There was a pause as Tolley stared first into Hugh's face, then at the gun he held. Tolley slid his hand inside his jacket pocket, and it came out with his card in it. He held it out.

Hugh said: "Will you read it, Grace?"

She took the card and studied it carefully.

"It looks all right. It *says* the Metropolitan Police Force and it's signed by someone called the Commissioner."

"Come in," Hugh said, still keeping his voice low.

He did not know why, but suspected that there might be hidden microphones; Cellini wouldn't give an instruction without a good reason.

"How did you know — " Tolley began.

"Come into the room, and we'll do some mutual explaining," said Hugh. He stood aside. "You go first, Grace."

That was the moment when a man's voice came from the passage which ran to and from the children's room. It was low-pitched and penetrating.

"None of you will go anywhere."

The man was only just visible, for he had a dark scarf over his face, and was wearing a dark suit. It was just possible to see that he was armed.

"Put that gun away," ordered Tolley, his voice stiff with official authority. "I am a police officer."

There was a flash of light from the gun. It showed the man's hand and arm and even the glint in his eyes. With a gasp, half-moan, half-sigh, Tolley slipped to the ground.

"Neil!" cried Grace. "Don't — "

"Which lovebird next?" sneered the man at the end of the passage. His voice, Hugh realised, was not unlike his own. "I was upstairs this morning," he said. "In the attic. Yours was quite a performance. *Very* romantic. Which of you goes next? Don't waste too much time, I'm in a hurry. What a pity about that nice Powell couple, they seemed so devoted. Do you think it was a suicide pact?"

"Neil, for God's sake — "

"You are wasting time appealing to my better nature," Neil Powell said. "I have none. Nor has Pebby. We had planned this so neatly but you were harder to kill than we expected, Buckingham. Do you know it took us four years of searching to find a man who looked sufficiently like me to pass muster?"

"Was it worth it?" Hugh asked.

"Was what worth what?"

"The fact that you would be on the run from the police for the rest of your life?"

"Oh, no, no," said Powell, and he actually laughed. "You have it all wrong. I have a nice little niche carved out for me in a pleasant foreign country where they are so grateful to Pebby and me for all the information we've been able to sell them. *Sell*, Buckingham, not give. We shall live in luxury for the rest of our lives. I have a nice little wife and the children waiting for me. All the comforts of home. And do you know what, Grace, I'm not one bit sorry for you. I haven't the slightest pity for you. I've learned to hate you. *Hate*."

He raised his gun.

Hugh thrust out his left arm, and pain shot through it. But there was strength enough to send Grace hurtling against the wall, and time enough for him to shoot Powell with the pistol which had been so nearly used on him. Powell gasped, staggered, then fell to his knees. Almost on the instant the street door was thrust open, lights flared, as men raced up the stairs. John Hardy was among them, and close behind him was Manny Cellini.

Hugh stood with his bruised arm about Grace, as he said: "It's all right, I don't think he's dead, but your other man may be. You need a doctor, an ambulance — "

He began to sway.

He felt himself lifted and carried into the room from which he had come, heard Hardy saying to Grace in firm, reassuring tones: "It's all right, Mrs. Powell, we have your children. We raided Nathaniel Pebblewhite's house just after he telephoned you, and they were there. Not really scared at all."

There was pain in his arm.

Grace's voice, low and desperate: "He's not hurt, is he? He's not wounded?"

"No, Mrs. Powell," Cellini said in a voice which just pierced the mists in Hugh Buckingham's mind, "he's all in, that's all. Suffering from sheer exhaustion. When you know about it all you'll understand. I — I am deeply grieved about your husband. I doubt very much whether he realises the significance of what he was saying, he was 'high' on some drug. I am sure — "

"Dr. Cellini," Grace Powell said, "he meant every word. But in a way, isn't it better? If I had even the slightest feeling left for him it would hurt much more than it does. Don't grieve for me. I'm much more worried about the children."

There was silence; except that someone was moving down the stairs, heavily, clumsily. And then Cellini asked what must surely have been the silliest question Hugh Buckingham had ever heard.

"Must they ever know?" he enquired.

"Of course they must know," Grace said with quiet vehemence. "It wouldn't be possible to deceive them, even if — even if it were morally right." She looked at Hugh, who was on the other side of the table from her, in Dr. Cellini's dining-room. It was the afternoon of the day after the shooting, and much had happened.

Neil Powell was dead; the bullet had touched his heart.

Chief Inspector Tolley was alive, with every chance of recovery.

The Powell children, told that both their mother and father were ill, were now with their grandparents.

Nathaniel Pebblewhite was under detention but had not been charged. There was a great deal of coming and going between the Department of Overseas Trade — Special Services, and Scotland Yard. Interpol was also deeply involved. The simple truth, Hardy had told Cellini, was that the Special Services branch of the Department was the Industrial Secrets Department, and that Pebblewhite and Neil Powell had sold secrets to several nations at the same time, secrets which enabled many of them to come out with products in which Great Britain should have had a good lead. The two men had planned that Powell should take the blame, when the truth leaked out, and would 'die'. Or, rather, someone impersonating him would die in his stead.

Buckingham.

As far as they could discover, Hardy had said, Doreen was not involved; only frightened of becoming involved with the police.

"We may never know why," Hardy went on. "Unless we get a lead to her from this affair, we're not likely to try. I can tell you one thing, though. The Department would very much like to hush the whole matter up. If the story breaks it will be one of the biggest spy scandals in modern times, and it will prevent the Special Branch and Intelligence from finding out who was involved overseas."

After a few moments Cellini had said: "You would like it to be Hugh Buckingham who died? Is that what you mean?"

"*I* would like the whole truth," replied Hardy. "But the powers that be — well, think about it."

Now, they were thinking and talking about it, and gradually one thing had become apparent; the greatest obstacle was that the Powell children should not be deceived.

"You mean, it is better that they should know that their father was a spy, a murderer in intent, that with Pebblewhite he hired assassins, that he planned to kill you, their mother? I have a deep respect for the truth, but a deeper one still for human beings. Tell me how this knowledge will help them, Grace."

She almost sobbed: "It isn't only that! They'd never be deceived, not for long, they — "

"Not if they were told their father had suffered a long

illness, overseas; that the illness had changed him? This need not affect you two, for the illness could be during the school term, while they are away. And you could teach Hugh all about them so that he would be familiar with their likes and dislikes, their foibles and their dreams." Cellini spoke as if this was the only possible thing to do; and as he finished he smiled at Hugh. "Would you find these things worth learning, Hugh?" When Hugh did not answer at once, he went on: "Would anyone miss you very much? Wouldn't you prefer your life with Grace to the life you have been living?"

Hugh said, huskily: "Prefer? I would give half my life's span. But — *can* it be done?"

"Legally?"

"Yes."

"I think nothing need be done," Cellini said. "The matter is of such great importance that your Will could be — "

"No need to worry about that," Hugh interrupted, gruffly. "I have always kept my money fluid and my land controlled by partnerships which can quite easily have changes of partners. That is no problem. The only problem is the children, and — "

He broke off, looking at Grace.

"And what?" asked Cellini.

"Grace," said Hugh Buckingham, "do you want this? Do you believe we could live together happily, deceive the children in their own interests?"

"I can tell you this," put in Cellini, "there is nothing wrong in the moral sense and nothing fraudulent in the legal sense."

He stopped, looking first at Grace, and then at Hugh. He felt quite sure that they had become oblivious to his presence, and so, without a word, he got up and left the room. In his study, he telephoned John Hardy, whose eager: "What have they decided?" showed the full significance of the decision, and the amount of pressure being brought by the authorities.

"I think you can be quite sure that the death certificate can be made out in the name of Hugh James Buckingham," Cellini told him, and was not surprised by Hardy's fervent:

"Thank God for that!"

They were waiting for the children to come home from school, just two months later; both were of an age when they wanted to come home by themselves, and they were due at almost any minute. Hugh — who was now Neil — put his arm round Grace and drew her towards him.

"Any regrets, sweetheart? Any at all?"

"I can't believe I've lived any other life," Grace told him, "and nor, I think, will the children."

He kissed her.

Dr. Cellini was sitting in his study, some four weeks later still, when the telephone bell rang. Goodness! This might be Felisa! He lifted the receiver eagerly.

"Dr. Cellini?" a woman asked; the voice was that of Grace Powell. She went on eagerly: "I had to tell you. Both the children have just gone back to school. There wasn't the slightest hint that they saw any change in their 'father'. Do you know what they told me?"

"No," breathed Cellini. "But I can't wait to hear."

"They said" — and there was laughter in her voice — "that as he grew older, Old Tiz was growing nicer and nicer!"

When he rang off, a few minutes later, Dr. Cellini was also laughing with a great joy.